Dark Circles

M.M. Hughes

Twisted Oak Publishing

ISBN 978-0-994056900

mmhughes8118@yahoo.com

To my dear friend D.L.
You inspired me to write.
RIP.

Chapter 1

"Red eyes and tears no more for you my love I fear"
"Red eyes and tears no more for you my love I fear"
"No more fear, no more fear I'm in love"

The lyrics left Claire's mouth as it did a hundred times before. She always listened to Black Rebel Motorcycle Club when she was getting ready to go out. It was her ritual. In her room and sitting in front of her mirror, she first applied cover up particularly over her crow's feet. There were just a few wrinkles, which was very typical for any 30-something year old. She put down her foundation and picked up her jet black eyeliner, which brought out her hazel eyes.

"Losing the reasons to breathe I never lived"
"I'm losing the reasons to breathe I never lived"
"Never lived, never lived I'm in love"

Claire rummaged through her makeup bag and picked up some pinkish-red eye shadow. She then added a bit of black eye shadow on the sides of her eyes. She started to feel really sexy, transforming into quite the fox. She sipped her wine, white not red so not to stain her teeth. Claire picked up the mascara, which she always hated putting on. Her eyelashes were so long that they touched the tops of her eyelids, and if they were mascara-laden they would often leave black marks; so she was careful not to blink too much before they dried. Since it was the middle of winter in Vancouver, Claire was pretty pale so she added a bit of blush. It was a nice neutral, rose colour so that she didn't look like one of the young hoes waiting in the line at Roxy's Club. This thought made her chuckle as she used to be one of them.

"These are my reasons the truth is never filled"
"These are my reasons the truth is never filled"
"I'm never filled, never filled I'm in love"

Claire untied her ponytail and fixed her part ensuring that it was slightly on the left side of her head. She picked up her straightner and passed it along her brown hair. No grey, not yet. Both of her parents didn't start going grey until they were in their 50s. Claire downed the rest of her wine and applied a dark red lipstick. She sat back and posed in the mirror, staring at herself to ensure that she looked good. She glanced over to the left and stared at the wall: *Degree in Medicine, Class of 2008.* Claire then leaned over and sniffed a line of coke on her makeup table. "Just a little confidence boost," she said to herself.

"Red eyes and tears no more for you my love I kill"
"Red eyes and tears no more for you my love I kill"
"Red eyes and tears"

She got up, turned the music off, grabbed her clutch and left her room. The taxi was waiting.

*****

"Claire!" a woman yelled.

"Claire!" she yelled again.

"For Christ's sake Megs, I'm right here," Claire finally replied.

Megs walked over to Claire, who was in the living room, and grabbed her arm taking her into her bedroom.

"What's wrong Megs?"

Megs looked distraught and closed her bedroom door. She sat down next to Claire on the bed and looked straight into Claire's eyes, "I need you to give me something."

"Megs, you need to clarify honey."

"I feel incredibly down Dr. Lalonde and I need you to make me feel good about myself."

Claire realised what her best friend was trying to get at, which amused her. "Are you having a hard time turning 30, Megs?"

"I think so," Megs replied.

"I'm older than you and I think you are being really silly, you just had too much to drink."

Megs' dark brown eyes squinted as she attempted to give Claire a dirty look.

"I know you have Valium and god knows what else, and if you really care about me having a great time at my own birthday party, you will give me something so that I can enjoy myself."

Claire met Megs when she was doing her undergrad at UBC. They were partnered up in a biology lab and just hit it off. Megs was such a natural at biology and excelled in botany. She was so good at growing shit, and she channelled that skill into a more entrepreneurial use and grew weed. Megs had a two-bedroom apartment and rented the second room out to a Miss Mary Jane. Mixed with her botanical skills and great business sense, she supplied weed to so many people at university including a couple of professors. Megs made such great money selling weed that by the time she graduated, financially she was in the black.

Meanwhile, the majority of the new graduates, who didn't have any parental financial support, were in debt up to their eyeballs. On the weed front, things were going really well for Megs until her final year. Her idiot ex-boyfriend was having a difficult time handling the "ex" part, so he threatened to tell the authorities if she didn't take him back. Megs couldn't take the chance, and as she was trying to smooth things over with *Jake the Jerk,* she was able to sell up what she could and destroy the rest. She had a good lump sum at the end of it and vowed never to do such risky things again. However, the taste of entrepreneurship was just too good, so she decided to use the lump sum for a more socially acceptable cause and started up a flower business. Her little flower shop slowly expanded, and she did fairly well in her first few years of business.

However, Megs had consistent problems with her main distributor. Her business, Rose Petals Flower Shop, was all about corporate social responsibility, which meant the flowers had to be sustainably grown, fairly traded, and not cut by a 9-year-old child in some developing country on the other side of the globe. Megs held these values close to her heart, but was constantly butting heads with the flower distributors who seemed to only care about profit.

Finally, she had enough and decided to be her own flower distributor. She was constantly flying to various South American countries, especially Colombia. Megs was meeting with various flower farmers developing partnerships with them. Within a year she had to rent out a warehouse with a large refrigeration unit to hold the flowers. There were so many pseudo-hippie areas in Vancouver such as Kitsilano that her Rainforest Alliance certified, sustainably grown and expensive flowers were a hit.

Claire knew from the beginning when Megs popped the drug question that she was going to give in. She always did no matter what they were arguing about. And Megs was so responsible that Claire had no real qualms about giving Megs a little pick-me-up. Claire was not a drug pusher, but she was a party girl. Most people in her circle of friends knew that she always had a supply of various prescriptions drugs in her purse with Valium and Vicodin being the most common.

"Megs, you sound like a desperate druggie who needs her next fix."

"I do, don't I?" Megs said.

Megs looked down at her hands.

"Oren is also starting to get annoyed with me and he told me to stop acting like an idiot."

"Because you feel anxious?" Claire asked.

"You're both right, I'm being stupid; but I can't help how I feel. It must be the alcohol, but I've only had half a bottle of wine."

Claire smirked at this drunken logic and carefully opened her clutch and unzipped the inside pocket. She didn't want Megs to see the bit of coke she brought purely for personal use. Megs would be so pissed if she found out.

"Here's some Valium, babes. You know the drill. If you start feeling dizzy or sick, let me know ASAP."

"Thanks Claire Bear," Megs said as she took the pill.

Megs popped the pill in her mouth and gave Claire a big hug.

"Megs, you are so beautiful. Always remember that. Hey, do you want your present?"

Megs clapped her hands together like a giddy little kid. "Of course I do!"

Claire pulled two tickets out of her purse and mischievously looked at Megs.

"Guess who?" Claire asked.

"You have to give me a clue. Which country are they from?"

"Our own," Claire replied.

"Brian Adams." Megs guessed.

They both laughed.

"C'mon Megs be serious."

"Okay. Black Mountain."

Claire shook her head. "Nope. They are instrumental and from Montreal"

Megs' eyes lit up. "Godspeed You! Black Emperor!"

"Yes ma'am," Claire said.

Megs leaned over and gave Claire a big hug. "What an awesome gift. Thanks hun."

"And I better be your number two, not Oren," Claire said.

"Of course not! He doesn't even like them. He hates music without lyrics," Megs replied.

"He's so cultured," Claire said sarcastically.

"Well, we better get back to my party." Megs then stood up, full of new confidence, and both girls left the bedroom.

Megs walked straight up to Oren and grabbed his ass and kissed him.

"Wow. You are really happy now. What did you and Claire talk about to put you back in a good mood?" Oren asked.

Oren grabbed Megs' wine glass and topped it up.

"She gave me my birthday present. Tickets to see Godspeed You! Black Emperor at the Vogue," Megs said.

"What the fuck kind of band name is that?" Oren asked.

"It's not that fiddle-dee-dee music that you like. And actually you have heard them before, and specifically told me to turn that apocalyptic shit off," Megs sweetly replied.

"So you are taking Claire, right?" Oren laughed.

Oren and Megs were dating for a few years and they lived together for one. He knew her well and loved her dearly. He noticed that something was indeed strange with her behaviour. He initially assumed that she smoked some weed, but he couldn't smell it on her. It was just the sweet aroma of Dior's Hypnotic Poison. He then suspected that Claire gave her something a bit more potent than words.

He leaned into Megs and whispered into her ear. "What did Claire give you?"

"What do you mean Oren?" Megs said in a low voice.

"One minute you were a pain in the ass, acting all anxious and stressy. You then go off with Claire and come back beyond relaxed. Remember, I'm a doctor, too. I'm not an idiot Megan." Oren raised his voice as he was getting extremely annoyed.

Megs took a deep breath as she tried to keep calm so that she didn't make a scene. "Look, chill out Oren, it's just Valium. Stop talking to me like I'm a child."

Megs was done with the conversation, so she stormed out of the kitchen and mingled with her other guests.

At that point Oren was on a mission to find Claire. He wasn't pissed off at Megs for taking the Valium. He was actually more curious than ever to find out why Claire, the most in-control and relaxed person on this planet, needed Valium. This whole situation seemed a bit suspicious. He left the kitchen on a mission to find Claire.

Megs and Oren lived in a two-bedroom condo, so it was going to be quite easy to locate Claire. He quickly looked in the living room but didn't see her. He checked the bedrooms but Claire wasn't in there, either. *She's probably in the closet fucking her next victim.* Oren thought to himself. Straight away he felt a bit guilty for thinking this way about one of his closest friends, but then again that woman was always looking to get laid. Oren went back into the living room and found Claire talking to a couple of mutual friends by the entertainment system. He wasn't sure how he missed her the first time. He walked over to the stereo, picked up his iPod, and changed the song to Home for a Rest from one of his favourite bands Spirit of the West. He then grabbed Claire who was reluctant to dance at first, but with Oren's persistence she gave in and he started swinging her around. After a few minutes others joined in. Drinks were flying and everyone was hooting and hollering. Even Megs was being passed around as she was the birthday girl. Oren didn't want Megs to be involved with his potential confrontation with Claire, so he took this opportunity to gracefully lead Claire into the now quiet kitchen.

"Another drink?" Claire asked.

Oren didn't say a word and just stared at Claire, which annoyed her. "What is it Oren?"

"Look, I know that you gave some Valium to Megs."

"Oren, she's an adult."

"That's not what concerns me," Oren said and he snatched Claire's purse and opened it up.

"What the hell are you doing? Give it back to me. You're being an asshole," Claire yelled, but no one could hear them because Spirit of the West was blaring out of the speakers.

Oren turned around and opened up the inside pocket. He noticed the coke, but instead grabbed the bottle of pills.

Oren read the label on the bottle that was prescribed to Mallory Nixon. "Did you change your name recently?" he asked.

Claire grabbed the bottle and her clutch from Oren and as if it was perfectly timed Megs walked into the kitchen. Oren smiled at Megs and said. "Are you alright sweetie? You certainly were dancing up a storm."

Megs then looked at Claire, who also smiled. "We were just having a bit of a discussion regarding Oren's shit taste in music."

Megs didn't believe them and knew that they were probably arguing about the whole Valium incident. At this point she didn't care. She just wanted to have fun.

"Well, are you guys going to come and join the party or argue all night?" Megs asked.

*****

It was getting pretty late and most of the guests went home. After Oren finished putting Megs to bed, he sat down beside Claire on the couch.

"I'm not leaving until we talk," Claire said.

"Agreed," Oren replied.

10

Claire sighed and looked at Oren. "Mallory Nixon was one of my patients who recently died. She was terminally ill and I basically prescribed her anything she needed. The poor woman was in a lot of pain. She was also taking Valium for years. When she died her family didn't know what to do with her cocktail of drugs, so they gave them to me to dispose of them accordingly. And instead of handing them into a pharmacy, I kept them for recreational use. I'm not harming anyone."

Claire was about to say more, but didn't feel like she had to justify why she did this. So she closed her mouth and looked at Oren, waiting for him to respond.

"I'm not interested in why you stole the prescriptions or how you rationalise your decision to steal them in the first place. I'm just completely floored how easy it was to do so."

Claire looked at Oren in disbelieve. "Are you being sarcastic?" Claire asked.

Oren rolled his eyes, sat back and crossed his legs.

"Perhaps I'm too ethical, and I'm tired of being so ethical all the goddamn time," Oren replied.

Claire looked at Oren straight in the eyes. "Stop beating around the bush."

"Claire, did you ever think about how much money you could make if you sold these drugs at parties rather than handing them out like candy?"

"No, of course not." Claire sipped on her nearly empty glass of wine. "Firstly, I would never charge my friends money for prescription drugs that I stole."

"Secondly?" Oren asked.

"Well, I wouldn't even know what to charge. Ten bucks per pill? Twenty? Thirty? And the amount drugs that I could take, not steal, wouldn't even equate to a night out." Claire put down her empty wine glass. She knew where Oren was going with this conversation and she wanted none of it.

"How much money do you owe Claire?" Oren asked.

"A lot," Claire replied.

"I owe 60 grand Claire."

"Wow, lucky you, I owe 80." Claire grabbed her clutch and stood up.

"I'm tired Oren, call me a taxi. My phone is dead."

Oren picked up his cell and called Yellow Cab. After he put down his phone he looked at Claire.

"I just want you to think about what we talked about tonight. Really think about. That's all I ask."

Claire nodded, grabbed her coat, and walked downstairs. She didn't even want to wait for her taxi in the same room as Oren. Instead, she decided to wait in the foyer. She wasn't annoyed at Oren. Claire's head was spinning and she just wanted to be alone.

Chapter 2

After a few days since Megs' birthday, Claire still couldn't stop thinking about the conversation she had with Oren. Her lifestyle was indeed very affluent, and she found it quite difficult to pay off her student debt. Claire was a spender. The day she finally became a licensed doctor she decided to buy a BMW as a gift to herself. She always wanted a black convertible, so she opted for a 135i M sport version. Claire's credit cards were always maxed out. When she paid one of her credit cards off, she often felt that it is time for another holiday, new clothes or more nice furniture. She tried to budget herself, but she loved buying shit. Claire was the definition of consumerism and she was very materialistic. That spending attitude pissed Megs off, as she had quite the opposite view regarding this subject matter, and she constantly lectured Claire about irresponsible consumerism.

"Dr. Lalonde," a nurse said as she peeked her head into Claire's office. Claire looked up and smiled.

"I'm sorry to bother you about this, but one of the patients refuses to have any of the nurses' conduct a pap test and she is asking for a doctor to do it instead."

"Did she say why?" Claire asked.

"She doesn't trust nurses, we apparently hurt her," the nurse replied.

"You got to be kidding me. You've done paps millions of times more than I have. So how did I get stuck with this patient?" Claire laughed.

"You're the only female doctor here," the nurse replied.

"No worries Laura, I love difficult patients, especially at the end of my shift," Claire said sarcastically.

Claire walked into the treatment room where a middle-age woman was sitting patiently on the hospital bed. She looked up to Claire and asked "Are you a doctor?"

"Yes, I am. My name is Dr. Lalonde." Claire put on some latex gloves. "You do realise that nurses are more than qualified to carry out pap tests," Claire said.

The patient just shrugged.

"Can you please take off your pants and underwear and put this sheet overtop of you. Just let me know when you're ready," Claire said as she pulled the curtain over.

As Claire waited for the patient, she started to think about her conversation with Oren again. Hundreds of patients come and go at a walk-in clinic. She already lost count of how many patients she saw that day.

"I'm ready."

Claire grabbed the speculum and opened the curtain.

"Aren't you going to warm that up?" the patient asked.

"We don't use metal speculums any more, this is plastic," Claire replied.

The patient laid down and positioned herself as though she had done this many times before.

"Can you shift your bum a bit forward?" Claire asked.

Claire put her hand on the patient's knee. "Are you ready?"

The patient nodded and began breathing deeply but she seemed to be in control.

Claire put the speculum inside her.

"Okay, now relax. I'm now going to take a swab inside your cervix."

As Claire performed the pap test her mind wandered. She couldn't just steal medication because they always did inventory. But how would they keep track of all her patient's prescriptions? Or even the patients that she sees? The majority of the patients that would go to the clinic she would only see once, especially the out-of-towners. What is the chance of a patient coming back for a second time that comes from Kelowna, or another province or another country for that matter? All these questions made Claire feel more confident in Oren's idea.

"Is everything alright down there?" the patient asked.

"Oh sorry, I was just making sure that I got enough cells. We wouldn't want to call you in here again." Claire lied as she gently took the speculum out. The poor patient was left with her legs spread apart a little longer than usual because of Claire's wandering mind.

*****

Megs was reading the Vancouver Sun and sipping her vanilla latte in a cafe while waiting for Claire. She knew all too well the nature of walk-in clinics and remembered to bring something to read while she waited for Claire. Twenty minutes went by before Claire finally burst through the cafe doors.

"Oh my god, I'm so sorry Megs! It was so busy in the clinic today."

Megs looked at Claire and smiled. "I know how it is Claire Bear. I was just chilling and reading."

Claire went over to the counter and ordered an Americano. A few minutes later she joined Megs at her table. "So how was your day?" Claire asked.

"Forget the small talk, something has been on my mind since my party, and I really need to talk about it," Megs said.

"Oh," Claire said as she put down her coffee cup.

Only one word left Megs' lips. "Oren."

Claire rolled her eyes. "Is this about the Valium thing? You know he doesn't give a shit."

"Well, he certainly seemed to give a shit. And it's not just that incident, there have been many. Sometimes I feel like I'm dating my father. One minute he's lecturing me and the next he's being all passionate and touchy. It's weird," Megs said.

"You know he loves you. He's just a bit of a control freak," Claire said.

15

Megs shook her head. "I don't know if I can take this Claire. I just want a simple relationship. No more mind games."

"You guys are great together. He loves you. I would have never set you up with someone who I didn't trust. You know his history. After his mother died, his father became a recluse and wouldn't even leave the house to buy groceries. Not only is he an only child, but he had to look after his father instead of doing normal teenage things," Claire said.

Megs shrugged her shoulders and sighed, but Claire persisted. Megs and Oren are two of her closest friends and she just couldn't bear to see them break-up.

"Look Megs, his personality is what feeds his drive. And if it wasn't for his drive, god only knows where he would have ended up after essentially losing both of his parents. Think about how he put himself through university. How he became a doctor. It's amazing what he achieved, and he could have only done it with that stubborn and controlling personality of his."

Claire sipped her coffee and kept going.

"And think about how he needs you. Megs, you calm him down and ground him. Opposites attract. Instead of breaking up with him, perhaps you could talk to him," Claire said.

"Okay Claire. I get your point. And for the record, I never said I wanted to break up with him. I was just sharing my frustration with his over-controlling personality. It's starting to push me away," Megs said.

"Well, why don't you talk to him about it?" Claire asked. "Oren is a reasonable guy."

"Damn straight I'm going to talk to him about it. I just wanted to discuss this with you first. Sometimes a girl needs a second opinion, especially from her best friend."

Claire smiled with relief. "You know I'm always here for you Megs."

"Thanks Claire Bear."

"I'm starving; did you want to get some food?" Claire asked.

"Sorry Claire, I had a late lunch and I also promised Oren that I will have supper ready for him tonight. It's my turn and he's working until 8 p.m."

"So you're planning to fill his belly with goodness before giving him the third degree?" Claire laughed.

"Well, kind of." Megs smiled, stood up and started to put on her coat. "I better go to the grocery store."

"It's not even 5 o'clock. What's the rush?" Claire asked.

"Sorry hun, I need some alone time. You know, think about what to say tonight. My mind is all over the place right now." Megs bent down and kissed Claire on the cheek. "I will call you in the morning. Try to be a good girl tonight, it's not even midweek."

"I have a hospital shift first thing in the morning funny girl. Early night for me," Claire said.

Claire waved good-bye to Megs as she left the cafe and started to read the front page of the Sun. She also wanted some time alone to think about her conversation with Oren at Megs' birthday party more seriously. However, brainstorming with Oren would have to wait a couple of days. Claire smirked at the thought of Megs giving Oren shit. She knew that their initial conversation would most likely turn into a full-blown argument. Those two were so damn stubborn, and neither would back down. Eventually Megs would get through to him. She always did. Megs may be short, but her presence in any room always commanded attention, especially with the boys. Not only did she have her mother's gorgeous looks and out-of-control curly hair, she also had her so-called Latin American temperament.

It's actually quite funny seeing her stand beside Oren because physically, they were complete opposites. He was over a foot taller than Megs with blond hair and blue eyes. You could be sure that they would have made beautiful babies. Claire stopped mid-thought. She started questioning why she always tried to prevent Megs from breaking up with Oren. It wasn't the first time Megs came to her with similar relationship woes. Claire quickly shook that thought out of her head and focussed back on her conversation with Oren.

She grabbed a pen from her purse and started to jot down how many times she prescribed an opioid narcotic pain reliever in the past several weeks. She couldn't remember every detail, but she did note that each week differed vastly. Claire was mainly based at the walk-in clinic, but she also did shifts at the hospital. She thought about working at the medical centre in Downtown Eastside again. They handed out methadone like candy in that part of Vancouver. Claire ripped the note-filled page off the newspaper and shoved it in her purse. She would have to wait until the weekend to speak with Oren, after things hopefully chilled out between him and Megs.

Claire stood up and put her jacket on. She was getting really hungry and decided to go via Win's to pick up a number 35 on her way home. God she had such a thing for black bean sauce.

Chapter 3

"Man, I'm hungry!" Oren said to a resident as he grabbed his patient's file. "It's getting pretty close to 7 p.m. and the waiting room still looks pretty full."

"We stopped accepting patients over two hours ago," the resident said. "And I have no clue how we'll manage to get through all of these people in the next hour. Looks like it's going to be another late one." The resident doctor smirked. Oren knew very well that he often does double shifts at various hospitals, and considers walk-in clinics to be a day off.

"Well then, James, are you going to do something productive tonight?" Oren asked.

"As lame as it sounds, I have a date with my remote control and my bed. I've basically worked nonstop for a few weeks now, you know how it is as a resident," James replied.

"All too well, and once you're a licensed doctor, it doesn't get much better," Oren said and he quickly walked towards the examination room.

Just as Oren turned the corner, he bumped into his colleague Terry with so much force that he fell on top of him.

"Ah shit, sorry Terry," Oren said as he helped him up.

"Don't worry about it. We need to mount a mirror on the wall so that we can see who's coming around the corner." Terry laughed.

Oren patted Terry on the back and went into an examination room.

As he introduced himself to the patient he put on some latex gloves and noticed blood on his palm. He quickly removed the gloves and washed his hands. The blood wasn't his. He wondered if he somehow hurt Terry when they fell. He put on a new pair of gloves and started examining the patient's foot. The foot-care clinic ran from 3 p.m. to closing, which accounted for many of the patients who were waiting to be seen. Oren was relieved as he realised that most of the patients would be receiving treatment for their stubborn plantar warts; and he would just have to do a quick check up after the foot technician was done with them before they could leave the clinic. Closing at 8 seemed to be achievable once again.

*****

Oren was sitting in his office finishing up some paperwork. He was right; most of the patients were there for the foot-care clinic. It was just after 8, and he was really looking forward to Megs' home-cooked meal.

Terry walked into the office. "Hey Oren, are you almost ready to go?"

"Nearly, just a few more minutes," Oren replied.

"James has a few more things to do so he offered to close the clinic tonight," Terry said.

Often Terry and Oren would take the Sky Train together since they lived in the same direction.

Just as Terry was about to leave the office Oren noticed blood on his lab coat, so he reached out and grabbed it for a closer inspection.

"Hey, what the hell are you doing?" Terry asked as he pulled his lab coat out of Oren's hands and backed away. Oren then noticed blood on Terry's pants as well.

"You're bleeding," Oren said as he pointed at his leg.

"It's nothing! I must have spilled some blood or something," Terry said.

"Sorry man. I'm done here now. Let's go," Oren said and he removed his own lab coat and put on his jacket. Terry did the same and they both left the clinic.

For the duration of their walk to the station, as well as the Sky Train ride, nothing was mentioned about the blood. They mostly talked about the Canucks and if they will make the playoffs again this year. Terry's stop was first so he left Oren alone with his thoughts. Oren realised he was being quite aggressive when he grabbed Terry's lab coat to examine the blood, and he was actually a little embarrassed by it. Terry was about five years older than him, and they worked together since they were resident doctors. Terry was a great doctor and Oren had the utmost respect for him. He would even trust him with his own mother.

It was Oren's stop and he disembarked the train and started walking home. As he opened the door he could smell Megs' delicious food. Both Oren and Megs took turns cooking, and they both can hold their own in the kitchen. And on that particular night he was so thankful that she came home early. Being a business owner, Megs often came home quite late, especially on special occasions like Valentine's or Mother's Day. And he was not into eating take-out once again. That happened all too frequently with their crazy schedules.

"Hey babe! It smells so damn good in here," Oren said and he walked over to Megs and gave her a passionate kiss. He was so happy to be home and in her arms.

"Well, I hope you're hungry because I went to town tonight and cooked up a storm." Megs smiled.

Megs brought the food over to the table. Oren was salivating at the sight of the breaded chicken breast, eggplant bake, spaghetti squash and Caesar salad.

As they sat down and ate their supper, they talked about each other's day. Oren started to talk about Terry and the blood incident. "I feel so embarrassed, Megs."

Megs couldn't believe that Oren just admitted to wrongdoing. And in that second she decided to put her heavily rehearsed argument regarding Oren's control issues on the backburner.

"I really don't think you should worry about it Oren. Terry has so much going on in his life right now that he probably already forgot about it," Megs said.

Oren smiled. "You're right Megs. Poor guy. He won't even talk about it."

"Did you try?" Megs asked. "I know how you guys are when it comes to pouring out your feelings to one another."

"It doesn't happen," Oren said. "But I'll try when I feel the timing is right."

Megs was right. Terry had a lot on his mind and he was going through quite the dirty divorce. He was a workaholic and was barely home; his wife felt neglected and had found comfort with their neighbour. Terry can't prove it, but he was fairly certain that his wife was screwing their neighbour in their own home while their 3-year-old son was sleeping under the same roof. He confronted his wife about his suspicion, and she admitted to having an affair. She told him that she didn't love him anymore. He left and she tried to take him to the cleaners.

"Do you know when the court date is?" Megs asked, as if she was reading his train of thought.

"Not sure. Soon I suppose," Oren replied.

Oren touched Megs' hand and looked into her eyes. "I promise that I will always put you before work."

"Me too," Megs said.

As they started to clear up, Megs was feeling a lot better about her relationship with Oren. Claire was right; they were good for each other.

Chapter 4

It was an insanely busy week and Oren was so relieved that it was Friday. He was sitting in front of the TV clicking through the channels, and finally decided to settle with reruns of Breaking Bad. He was eating his re-heated Thai green curry from the previous night when his cell rang. The first thing that jumped into his mind was that he was getting called in to do a shift at the hospital. He debated whether or not to answer it until he saw Rose Petal's Flowers pop up. "Hey gorgeous."

"Hey babe. It looks like I'm going to be here until midnight at the earliest. The shipment is here, but everything is messed up. I've gotten flowers that I didn't even order and the flowers that I did get aren't even the right ones," Megs said.

"Did you want me to come down there and help out?" Oren asked.

"Oh goodness no! You've had such a crazy week. And it's nothing I can't handle. Two of my staff are in too. Please don't worry about it," Megs replied.

"What are you going to do about this screw up?" Oren asked.

"Well, I can't exactly call up my farm in Colombia and give them shit. And these flowers are beautiful. I'm sure I can sell them. It's all about marketing anyways. I'll visit my main consumers tomorrow, but I'm certain they will go for these too," Megs said.

"Seriously though, let me know if you need any help. I'm cheap labour!" Oren laughed.

"Oh, I'm sure you'd get me to repay you in a non-monetary form though," Megs said.

"That's right little lady!" Oren said.

"On another note, what are you going to do tonight then?" Megs asked.

"Actually, I won't be lonely. Claire is coming over after her shift armed with a greasy pizza," Oren replied.

"You've been eating on the phone the whole time we've been chatting, which I might add is a little on the rude side," Megs said.

"I'm starving, so I'm eating a bit of the leftover curry from last night. I can listen and eat at the same time. The only casualty is my cell phone. So remind me to clean it later," Oren said.

"Okay smart-ass, I have to go. I'm assuming Claire will be there by the time I get home. I know how you two winos are," Megs said.

"Red wine and greasy pizza. We're living on the edge tonight," Oren laughed.

"Okay babes. See you later. Love you," Megs said.

"Love you too and good luck!" Oren said.

*****

Oren's heart nearly jumped out of his body when he was abruptly woken up from the sound of the doorbell. Oren looked at the clock and he was actually only dozing for 10 minutes. He got up from the couch and buzzed Claire in. A few minutes later Claire busted into the door with a couple of boxes of pizza and a bottle of wine.

"Shit Oren. Did you just wake up or something?" Claire asked.

"Thanks Claire," Oren said sarcastically as he looked in the mirror in the hall. "And yes, I was napping on the couch. I had a hectic week."

Claire rolled her eyes. "Isn't that the name of the game? I've never had a relaxing week at work as a doctor." She did not sympathise with Oren at all.

"Jesus Claire. Chill out on me. You've only been here for two minutes and I'm nearly in tears." Oren laughed as he gave Claire the finger. Claire and Oren were more like brother and sister. Megs always thought that they treated each other like siblings because they were both the only children in their families. It also amazed Megs how two intelligent and educated people could engage in such filthy dialogue. They called each other names and beat each other up. Megs hoped that those two child-like adults would never work in the same clinic because she didn't think they had the ability to act professional towards each other.

Oren grabbed the bottle of wine out of Claire's hand and she slammed the two boxes on the kitchen counter. "The Hawaiian is for the freak who likes pineapple on his pizza and the Canadian is for a flesh-eater like me."

"Good luck with that large Claire. I doubt you could even eat three slices."

"I'm h-angry! So I'll give it my best shot," Claire said.

"Well, that explains why you've been a bitch since you got here," Oren said.

"Fuck you Oren," Claire said jokingly as she loaded a couple of slices on her plate. Oren and Claire then moved into the living room and sat on the couch. Claire's facial expression became very serious as she looked directly into Oren's eyes. "I've been thinking about what we talked about last weekend, and I think you're onto something. I truly believe that we could make a lot of money selling prescription drugs."

"Well, I've been thinking about it, too, and I've found many holes in my original idea," Oren quickly replied.

Claire swallowed her mouthful of pizza. "You are confusing me, Oren. When you have an idea as good as this one you get obsessed and figure out how to fill the holes."

Claire sipped her wine. "So you don't want to do it anymore?"

"I'm not necessarily saying that I don't want to do this. I just think we need to rethink our original plan." Oren got up to grab another pizza slice from the kitchen. "Stealing drugs from the clinics and hospitals isn't going to work. You know that Claire. All the good stuff is under lock and key and carefully monitored." Oren sat back down. "And I think if we did steal the drugs from various clinics we'd be found out really quickly."

Claire nodded her head in agreement. "And it's not like we have an ongoing supply of dead patients, either."

"Exactly!" Oren said.

Claire raised her eyebrows. "So what do you propose to do Dr. O'Brian?"

"Write prescriptions in return for money," Oren replied.

"Doctors get caught for that shit all over the world. They have their license suspended and are thrown in jail," Claire said.

"We're not going to get caught." Oren topped up his empty wine glass. "First and foremost, we can't get greedy. We need to be selective and careful. We must keep track of all our pseudo-patients, including their addresses and which pharmacies that they go to."

Claire was skeptical. "And that's how most of those doctors got caught. It was almost always the pharmacist who became suspicious and reported it to the police."

"Exactly Claire. A pharmacist recognises that Dr. Smith is writing prescriptions for a high number of patients for opioids such as Vicodin, methadone, fentanyl, oxycodone and so on. So the pharmacist reports him, which in turn triggers an investigation."

"Well, we can't do that shit out of our own clinics. And I'm not doing it from the trunk of my car in a Save on Foods parking lot either," Claire said.

"Of course not. Neither of us have our own clinic. This is the perfect opportunity to start one up," Oren said.

Claire shook her head. "Then we're traceable Oren."

"Well, then you suggest something rather than shooting down my ideas all the damn time." Oren was getting frustrated with Claire's negativity.

"Gear down there big shifter! I'm playing devil's advocate. We're not exactly planning something as fail safe as a birthday party. And if we get this wrong, we're going to jail." Claire crossed her arms. "You are on to something. We need to have both legit and pseudo-patients. And a temporary clinic may be the way to go."

"Temporary for sure. If we do this too long we'll inevitably get caught," Oren said.

"We need a fluffy front so that we don't have to spend loads of money on equipment." Then an idea hit Claire so hard that she couldn't contain her excitement. "Homeopathy!"

"Homeopathy?" Oren asked. "And what the hell do you know about it?"

"I wrote a couple of papers about how it is complete bullshit and trust me, I did my research," Claire replied.

"So is there a crash course or something that I can take in this so-called science?" Oren said.

"Tomorrow I'll email you my research papers. Whenever I prove that a remedy is utter bullshit, pretend the opposite holds true."

"Sound good. But what if one of our legit patients comes back with the same ailment?" Oren asked.

"Placebos work nearly 90 percent of the time," Claire replied.

Oren laughed. "Ninety percent? Sounds like you're the one who's being too optimistic now."

"Whatever Oren. We're not going to stock homeopathic medication in the clinic. Well, maybe the basics. I don't know." Claire slumped back into her chair.

"Chill out Claire. We don't need to figure out all the answers tonight. We've only just formulated the idea." Just as Oren finished his sentence his cell started ringing. He picked it up right away thinking it was Megs. "Hey babes."

"Hey good-looking. I've been thinking about you all evening," a male voice said.

"Hey Alex. Sorry man. I assumed it was Megs," Oren said.

"No worries. That was the highlight of my very shitty night." Alex said.

"What's up?" Oren asked.

"I need you to do me a massive favour. My wife had to leave town tonight because her mother was rushed to the hospital and it doesn't look good. She had a stroke. And since this is so last minute, I can't find a babysitter for my kids," Alex said.

"Sorry to hear about your mother-in-law," Oren replied. "So do you want me to babysit or take your shift tomorrow?"

Alex started laughing on the other end. "Aren't you allergic to kids?"

"It's no problem Alex. Thankfully the clinic closes early on Saturdays anyways. And it sounds like Megs has her hands full this weekend with her business."

"Thanks man. I'll take you and Megs out to dinner once this is all over."

"Did you want us to send some flowers to the hospital or something?" Oren asked.

"Thanks for the offer but you've done enough," Alex replied.

Oren hung up the phone and walked back into the living room.

"Shitty. Sounds like you're working tomorrow," Claire said.

Oren shrugged his shoulders. "Yeah. Not sure if you got the gist of the conversation, but Alex's mother-in-law had a stroke and she may not recover. As much as I wanted to tell him to stuff it, my emotional side got in the way."

"You sound like such a dick," Claire said.

Claire got up and put her dishes in the kitchen. "Well, it's after midnight and you have to work in the morning." Claire grabbed an unopened bottle of wine from Oren and Megs' wine rack. "Tempranillo. Nice!"

"Help yourself Claire," Oren said sarcastically.

"Well, I don't have to work tomorrow, the booze stores are closed and I only have hard liquor at home. It's probably best that I stick with wine tonight," Claire said.

"Are you going to cab it or take the Sky Train?" Oren asked.

"Well, I was going to wait until Megs got home and ask her to give me a lift," Claire replied.

"That would mean sleeping on the couch for a few hours. It's going to be a late one," Oren said.

"I know. I called her this afternoon. I even offered to help, but she wouldn't have any of it," Claire said as she put on her coat.

"I only had half a bottle of wine. I'll take the Sky Train."

Oren also put on his jacket. Claire knew all too well that it didn't matter how much she persisted that she can walk by herself, Oren would have to escort her to the station. That argument was lost many years ago.

Chapter 5

It was a typical Saturday at the clinic. For the first few hours in the morning it was fairly quiet, but by 11 a.m. patients were trickling in. Oren never bothered to take a lunch break if he was working on a Saturday because the clinic closed at 4 p.m. He always had scores of cashews in his desk to tide him over.

"Hey," James said as he poked his head into Oren's office. "I need to talk to you." Without waiting to hear Oren's response James closed the door and sat down. "Do you find that Terry is acting a bit strange today?"

Oren took advantage of the slow start in the morning and spent most of it in his office catching up on some paperwork. He didn't even say much to Terry other than a quick hello. Although, he did notice that Terry's black hair was dishevelled and he looked extremely tired. More so that day as the dark circles around his eyes were more pronounced than usual.

"Well, he looks tired and unkempt, but he hasn't been able to sleep much since the separation," Oren replied.

"Look. I know we need to be tolerant about that, but maybe it's time he takes a few days off. He almost seems confused. The patients don't have much confidence in him," James said.

"Don't be too hard on him. His job is keeping him sane right now. I'll keep an eye on him," Oren replied.

Oren got up and followed James out of the office; he spotted Terry talking to one of the nurses. He looked out in the waiting room and saw that the room was nearly full, but not as jam-packed as on a normal weekday. This didn't surprise Oren as he believed that most people had no qualms with taking a day off work to see a doctor, but those same people would no way in hell forfeit a few hours of their precious weekend. So Oren thought that those who were in the waiting room sincerely needed to be seen by a doctor. Oren wanted to leave on time, so he hopped back on the rotation with a new burst of energy and was ready to face patients with their various ailments.

*****

It was nearing the end of the day and Oren was relieved that so far all of his patients' problems were pretty much straightforward. His last patient was worried about a separated shoulder injury as it was still causing him a lot of pain after six months. So Oren solved that problem by giving him a doctor's note to see a physiotherapist. *Nice and easy* thought Oren. As he walked out of the examination room he heard a loud crash, and rushed into the clinic's small lab. Terry had accidentally knocked over a handful of urine samples, which were on the table; and a few of the sample's lids popped off.

"Jesus, Terry. There's piss everywhere!" Oren exclaimed.

James was also in the doorway. "Don't worry about it. I'll clean it up and call the patients back who need to give us another sample." James gave Oren a hard stare.

"Hey Terry. Can we have a quick chat?" Oren asked.

"Sure Oren, but I have to clean this mess up first," Terry said.

"No seriously. I will clean it up. It's not a problem," James said.

Oren followed Terry into his office.

"Is everything okay?" Oren asked.

"Yes. Actually no," Terry said and Oren grabbed his shoulder.

"Is it about the separation? Do you want to talk about it?" Oren asked.

"No. Look Oren. I appreciate that you are concerned, but I will be fine. I just didn't sleep very well last night," Terry said.

"Well, how about you just chill out in your office for a bit and get yourself together." Oren suggested.

"Yeah. You're right. Just give me 20 minutes or so. I'll be fine," Terry said. So Oren got up and left Terry alone, closing the door behind him.

James came up to Oren straight away.

"Is everything okay?" James asked.

"I don't know, but Terry is taking a few minutes out in his office. Apparently, he's just tired," Oren replied.

"So it's just me and you?" James asked.

"Let's get 'er done," Oren replied as he clapped his hands together. "I still want to go home at a decent time."

"You and me both. I need to sleep a few hours before going to the hospital to do a night shift," James said.

*****

The last patient left the clinic about 45 minutes after the official closing time and Oren ordered James to go home. "I don't have to work tonight and you do. Don't argue with me kid," Oren said with a smile.

Oren went back into his office to finish up some paperwork. Just as he sat down a nurse popped her head into the door. "Did Dr. Wu leave? I have a few things he needs to sign and he isn't answering his door."

"Did you try to open it?" Oren asked assuming that Terry did leave.

"Of course, but its locked," the nurse replied.

At that instant Oren bolted up from his chair, ran over to Terry's office and started knocking frantically on the door. "Hey Terry, are you in there?" Oren raised his voice. "Open up Terry." And at that instant he started kicking the door, which gave in pretty easily. Terry was slumped over his desk and he seemed to be passed out, so Oren started to shake him. "Wake up Terry!" Oren yelled. Terry started to move and raise his head, and both the nurse and Oren helped him over to the examination table and laid him down. Terry's breathing was erratic and he had a fever. Terry looked at Oren and mouthed the words "sepsis".

"Why the hell would you have a blood infection?" Oren asked. Terry looked at the nurse.

"Could you put together an IV? It looks like he has sepsis. He needs fluids." The nurse nodded and quickly left the room.

"You can't tell anyone. I've been injecting," Terry whispered.

"Don't say anything. We'll talk about this once you're stable," Oren said.

Oren left the room and intercepted the nurse who was preparing the IV. "Is there anyone else here?" Oren asked.

"No it's just us," the nurse replied.

"Terry let a nasty cut go septic," Oren lied. "And the rest is history."

"That explains why he has been acting so strange today," the nurse said. Oren looked at the nurse with astonishment. He was so wrapped up with wanting to finish early that he didn't take any notice of Terry, but everyone else did. Oren felt ashamed because he may have been able to catch this earlier.

"I'll insert this IV. The oxygen tank is pretty bulky and it's in the back," the nurse said.

By the time Oren dragged the oxygen tank into Terry's office, the nurse had already inserted the IV and she had packages of antibiotics spread out on the desk.

"I'm not sure which one you want to go with, but these are all we have in the clinic," the nurse said and she grabbed an oxygen mask and placed it over Terry's mouth.

"Hey Terry, can you hear me?" Terry opened his eyes and nodded. "I'm going to give you a couple of different types of antibiotics, do you agree with that?" Terry nodded yes and closed his eyes. His breathing was already returning to normal.

"I think he's stabilizing," Oren said. The nurse looked relieved. "There's nothing else you can do here, you should go home." The nurse was about to object, but Oren interrupted her. "Karen, you've done a great job. I really appreciate your help, but it's just a waiting game now. Please go home."

"Don't you think he should go to the hospital though?" Karen asked.

Oren was certain that if he took Terry to the hospital, they would find out that he was injecting and his license would be suspended; and he would most likely go to jail. And on top of what was going on with the separation, he couldn't let that happen.

"What we did for him in here is all what they can do at the hospital." Oren looked down at Terry. "He's going to be okay Karen."

Karen nodded, but she still didn't look convinced.

"Trust me on this," Oren said.

Karen stood up and was about to walk out the door when Oren walked up to her and put his hands on her shoulders. She was about half his size. "Please Karen, don't tell anyone about this. Terry is going through a rough separation and he's under a lot of stress. I'll make sure he takes a couple of days off at the very least." Karen smiled. Although she just started working at the clinic, she felt that she could trust Dr. O'Brian.

*****

After about an hour Terry was awake and was sitting up. Oren thought it was a good time to find out what the hell was going on.

"This looks really bad," Terry said.

"Yeah. You really scared us," Oren agreed.

"My life is so messed up Oren. I don't give a shit about Shelly. I don't think I would ever be able to forgive her. The thought of another man sticking his dick inside of her disgusts me, especially when Ethan was sleeping in the room next to them. What a sleazy thing to do."

Oren nodded and patiently waited for Terry to continue.

"I can't see my son when I want to see him. It's so screwed up Oren."

"Ethan adores you. And there is no reason why the judge won't grant you shared custody," Oren said.

"And the money. Do you know how much I already paid my lawyer?" Terry asked.

Oren shook his head.

"Lots! And the end is not in sight. Shelly is not only going after me for child support, which I have no problems in paying, but she wants alimony! Two grand a month! So I need to fight this."

"Surely she can't get much. She stopped working when Ethan was born." Oren was trying to reassure Terry, but he really didn't know much about marital disputes.

"He's nearly 3 years old!" Terry exclaimed.

"Look Terry. I know things in your life aren't going very well right now, but it doesn't explain why you are injecting god knows what," Oren said.

"Demerol, I've been injecting it straight into my muscles. Made me feel great when I had a broken leg a few years back, so I thought it would help me now," Terry said.

Oren thought back to when he bumped into Terry the other day. He had blood on his pants.

"You were injecting Demerol through your clothes?" Oren asked.

Terry nodded.

It was all coming together for Oren, but he never thought that Terry was the type to do such a thing. And although he didn't want to grill Terry too hard today, he had another question.

"How did you get the drugs?"

Terry looked down at his IV. "Can you take this out now?" he asked.

Oren put on a pair of latex gloves and started to remove the IV from Terry's arm.

"Free samples from pharmaceutical companies mostly." Terry put some pressure on his arm where Oren removed the IV to stop the blood. "They are always trying to pay us off to prescribe their shitty medicine, even if it isn't necessary. Most of those drug reps are evil scum bags, so I played them to get my fix."

"You just admitted that you are addicted," Oren said.

"I know. I am and after today I'm never going to touch that shit again. If it wasn't for you and Karen, god only knows what would have happened. I for sure would have gone into septic shock. Fuck, I may have never seen my son again." Terry's dark brown eyes were tearing up.

"You have to take some time off Terry. You nearly killed yourself," Oren said.

"I can't. When we don't work we don't get paid. And that means I can't afford to pay my lawyer, child support, and god knows what other hidden costs are coming up. And not to mention, I'm paying both a mortgage and rent right now. Not even my doctor's wage can cover all that. It's bad Oren. Really bad."

Oren sat back down and thought about the pseudo-clinic. He and Claire could do with another doctor. That's three different doctors writing prescriptions. Oren believed that they could bring in thousands of dollars per day, including the homeopathy patients. Homeopathy isn't covered by Canada's

Heath Care Insurance so they'd have to pay out of pocket, which means more profit for them. Claire was a genius for coming up with that idea.

"Well, aren't you going to say something Oren?" Terry asked.

Oren's wandering mind was brought back into the room. "I think I have a solution," Oren replied.

"What? Check myself into a loony bin and declare insanity? I wouldn't have to go to court then, and I probably wouldn't have to pay any support," Terry said.

"Look, it's probably the most inappropriate time to ask you after this scary ordeal, but you really need this," Oren said.

"Well, spit it out then," Terry said.

"Claire and I are thinking of opening up a homeopathic clinic where we would also write out prescriptions in exchange for cash."

Terry was dumbfounded. "What?"

"You know. We'd have real patients who are looking for holistic healing of some sort, and we'll also write out prescriptions for those who need real pain relievers."

Terry interrupted Oren. "You're right! It's a really inappropriate time to be offering me a position as a modern day drug dealer at your pseudo-homeopathic clinic! You're crazy Oren." Terry was far from impressed, and he slowly started to slide off of the examination table.

Oren tried to help him, but Terry shrugged him off. "Don't touch me man."

"Think about it Terry. Remember that doctor who was caught selling prescriptions for various opiates in front of a McDonald's? He was making $5,000 per night! Imagine how much we could make?"

Terry shook his head. "And imagine how long we'd spend behind bars if we get caught? First, I see the inside of a family court and then a criminal court. Doesn't sound like fun to me."

"And that's why we have to plan carefully." Oren started to worry that Terry might report him as he really didn't expect his reaction to be so negative.

"Forget it man. And you better keep this a secret," Oren stood up to leave the room. Terry made him feel like some dirty criminal and he hadn't even done anything yet.

"And you better keep my ordeal a secret, too. We now have something on each other," Terry said. He started walking towards the door and started to feel quite dizzy so he grabbed on to the chair.

"Megs has the car today so I will call you a cab. Do you even have any money to cover it?" Oren asked.

Terry sneered. "Yes I do."

"Sorry man, that was unnecessary," Oren said.

"There's a lot of emotion here right now. I just need to go home and rest. I'm taking a few days off, but no more. I need the money," Terry said.

"I'll write you a prescription for more antibiotics, but you should have enough for the next few days. Karen Leung thinks that you let a cut go septic," Oren said.

"Thanks for covering for me," Terry said.

"Well, what are friends for?" Oren said.

Oren could feel that the tension in the room clear, and he started to dial the number for a taxi.

"They'll be about 10 minutes. Do you want me to go home with you?" Oren asked.

"No. I'll be fine," Terry replied.

After Oren helped Terry into the taxi, he went back into the clinic and collapsed on a chair in the waiting room. Oren was exhausted. It was already dark out. He pulled his cell from his pocked and saw that he missed three calls from Megs, and one from Claire. He sent a text message to Megs to let her know that he would be another hour. He didn't feel like talking to anyone at that moment. He leaned his head back onto the wall and closed his eyes.

"What an insane afternoon," Oren whispered to himself.

Chapter 6

It was nearly 10 a.m. and Claire was perusing the internet. "No fucking way!" she said aloud to herself. Claire was doing research on how much homeopathy clinics charge. Forever Homeopathy, which was based in downtown Vancouver, charged $300 for the first two hours of a consultation and then a $125 for subsequent visits. And they generally included the price of their so-called medicine. Claire couldn't believe it.

There was a knock at the door so Claire put her coffee down and answered it. She knew it was Oren. They decided it would be best to plan the pseudo-clinic when Megs was at work; and since it was a weekday, they felt that it was the perfect opportunity to get together. Also, at noon they were looking at a rental just off of Commercial Drive in East Van. It was the ideal location as the demographic was perfect in that area of Vancouver. There were also enough holistic medical clinics around so they wouldn't draw attention to themselves. Claire felt good about this one. They already saw half a dozen rental spaces and quite frankly Claire was getting frustrated with Oren's pickiness.

"Hey! I've come armed with bagels of the Montreal kind," Oren said.

"Nice! Real bagels. Not that doughy shit that you eat here," Claire said and she grabbed the bag of bagels.

"Well, aren't you the Montreal snob," Oren said.

Claire went into the kitchen, put the bagels in the toaster oven and poured Oren a cup of coffee.

"You won't believe what I found out," Claire said.

"Something good I hope. I really need some good news right now," Oren replied.

Claire was a bit confused with what Oren meant by that, but she ignored it and kept going.

"Homeopathic clinics on average charge between $200 and $300 for the first consultation. And subsequent visits are anywhere between $80 and $150," Claire said.

"What about the herbal remedies?" Oren asked.

"Herbal remedies equate to little bullshit sugar pills. Didn't you read my papers yet?"

"Well. No, it's been a weird few days," Oren replied.

"I can pick some up. You can get them by the shiploads off the internet. I don't even mind hopping over the border and picking some up in Seattle. I'll sort that shit out. It won't be too expensive, especially if I get them in the States," Claire said.

Claire went into the kitchen and took the bagels out of the toaster oven. "I hope you like a lot of cream cheese."

"Don't go nuts with it! Sticks like you need more calories," Oren said and patted his belly. "I have to watch what I eat now. My metabolism isn't what it used to be." Claire rolled her eyes. It was true that Oren wasn't as skinny as he was when he was in his 20s, but he was far from being overweight. In her opinion he looked much healthier with his added couple of pounds than he did back when they were in university.

"I have to say Claire. Your idea of a homeopathy clinic as a cover-up is genius. It will also give us a chance to analyze the patients to ensure that we can trust them," Oren said.

"I'm not a complete idiot all the time," Claire said sarcastically.

Oren's cell started to ring.

"I hope you're not getting called in," Claire said.

Oren took his cell out of his pocket and saw that it was Terry.

"Not quite Claire but I have to take this," Oren said as he got up and walked into Claire's room so he was out of earshot.

"Hello," Oren said as he answered his cell.

"I'm in," Terry said.

There was a long pause since Oren was shock. "Are you fucking kidding me?"

"Look. I need this Oren. I'm financially screwed," Terry replied.

"How the hell can I trust you after your reaction the other day?" Oren asked.

Terry quickly snapped back. "You tried to bring me into the plot just after I was nearing septic shock. The timing sucked man."

Oren agreed with Terry, he should have waited a few days. "You have a point there. Sorry about that. I also wasn't thinking straight after seeing you in such a state."

"Yeah, it was pretty messed up. Thanks again for saving my life. I don't think I would have dragged myself to the hospital because of the injection issue. And I left it too long to treat myself," Terry said.

"That's another thing I'm worried about. I don't know if I want to do this with you if you are injecting the drugs we are trying to prescribe. It may impair your judgement," Oren said.

"You have my word Oren. Never again. And I haven't even craved any of that shit since." Terry took a deep breath. "Ever since I realised that I may have never seen my son again and that he would grow up fatherless."

"Okay listen... I'm at Claire Lalonde's house, and I haven't told her about bringing you into the plot," Oren said.

Terry knew Claire, but he didn't know her very well. He met her through Oren and they would often chat when they bumped into each other at parties or even at a doctor's conference. Since Terry was a family man, he often didn't go out; and when he did he was with his wife. And she didn't feel comfortable with him talking to single women, especially those as attractive as Claire.

42

"Potty-mouth Claire. Of course, she would be working with you," Terry said.

Oren laughed. "I'm sure she'd appreciate the nickname."

Oren was about to say good-bye when he remembered. "Listen, Megs doesn't know anything about this yet. Please keep it to yourself until I figure out a way to tell her."

"No problem Oren. My lips are sealed," Terry said.

"I'll call you once I tell Claire and we'll sort out a meeting to hash things out."

Terry agreed and they said good-bye.

Oren went back into the living room where Claire was glued to her laptop screen.

"More research?" Oren asked.

"Yeah, I think I should make an appointment with one of the homeopathy clinics so that I can experience it firsthand."

"Are you sure you want to fork out that amount of cash on such bullshit?" Oren asked.

"Absolutely, I'll just put it on my credit card. I want to get this right." Claire replied.

Oren sat down next to Claire on the couch.

"What do you think about having another doctor on our team?"

Claire looked up at him and shook her head. "Don't you think that would be too risky?"

"It's Terry Wu. He desperately needs the money. He's a trustworthy person," Oren said.

"I barely know him. We've chatted a few times and his wife scares the shit out of me," Claire said.

"You mean his ex-wife," Oren said.

"I hate to say it but in the long run he would be much happier. When Terry and I would talk to each other at a party or something, she would stare at us the entire time drilling holes into my head with her eyes. She's small, but deadly."

"Well, the bitch cheated on him with their neighbour and now she's taking him to the cleaners. Even with his doctor's wage he's unable to make ends meet."

"Don't they have a kid?" Claire asked.

"And that's another reason why he needs this. He needs this more than us. And think about how many more prescription we can prescribe?" Oren replied.

Claire sat back on the couch and thought about it. She trusted Oren's instinct. And having another doctor on board meant that they would make more revenue. Also, it would be safer. Another doctor's signature meant that pharmacists would be less likely to notice if a particular doctor is overprescribing opiates. Claire's wheels were turning.

"Okay Oren. I trust you; therefore, I trust your instinct. And if you think that Terry would be a good addition to our team then I agree."

Oren smiled. "Great. Now let's get the hell out of here and check out the rental."

*****

"Jesus!" Claire said as she slammed her empty shot glass on the table. "I hate tequila!"

Oren and Terry started laughing because Claire's disgusted face was priceless. Oren knew that Claire despised tequila, and when Terry brought the shots over he didn't say a word. Claire would never turn down a free drink.

"I'll never get tired of that face Claire bear," Oren said.

Claire gave Oren the finger as she chased the shot down with beer.

Earlier that day after they looked at the rental space, Oren phoned up Terry to see if he wanted to meet up at a bar to discuss the details of their plan. Within a few hours they were sitting at Falconetti's sharing a pitcher of beer, discussing details of their pseudo-clinic.

'No One Knows' started to blare out of Claire's purse on the back of her chair.

"Didn't know you smuggled Josh Homme in here? Now that is a man who'd I love to have a beer with," Oren said.

"Wow. I'm impressed you know who Queens of the Stone Age is," Claire said as she picked up her Blackberry.

"It's Middlestate Management," Claire said. "God, I hope we got the rental. I'm so sick of looking at places." Claire answered the phone.

"Hello, this is Dr. Claire Lalonde." Oren shook his head. He knew that Claire was trying to sound more professional to butter up the property owner.

"That's great news. Yes, we'll drop off a month's rent plus the deposit." Claire grabbed a pen out of her purse and wrote down an address on the back of a napkin. "Great. Thanks so much." Claire hung up and Oren picked up his pint of beer. "I'm assuming we got it." Claire nodded yes and also picked up her drink with Terry following suit. They cheered each other and drank their beer.

"Well, we certainly have a lot to do," Terry said.

"I know but I've been thinking so much about it," Oren said and he took the napkin in front of Claire and ripped it in half giving the side with the address back to Claire. "Since you're the main contact with Middlestate Management, can you sort out the keys and deposit? I'll transfer half of the money into your account and I'm assuming you can get the rest."

"I'll use my line of credit. I'm confident that we'll pay all this back in no time once our clinic is up and running," Claire said.

It was as if Oren was reading Terry's mind. "Terry, you don't have the cash."

"Don't worry. Claire and I can cover it." Just as Terry was about to oppose, Claire put her hand on his.

"You have enough on your plate Terry. And besides, we'll make this up in no time." Claire removed her hand from Terry's and looked at Oren. "What about medical equipment? Beds? Desks? Sphygmomanometer? Etcetera?"

"Terry and I will deal with that. We need those magic sugar pills that you mentioned in your paper. Unless Terry would do us the honours and teach us a bit about Traditional Chinese medicine?"

"That's such a stereotype!" Terry said, but he knew that Oren was just kidding.

"Typical Newfie. Assuming that all Chinese decedents believe in that hokey medical practice," Claire said in Terry's defence.

"What are you insinuating Claire? That all Newfies are whitewashed and racist?"

"No. Just naive because you are only surrounded by your drunken Celtic kin," Claire said.

"Ouch! You're just as bad as Oren now," Terry said to Claire.

"Claire always makes fun of Newfies, which I find very ironic since she's Quebecoise." Oren said in a really bad French-Canadian accent.

"I think you're misusing the word ironic Alanis," Claire said and punched Oren in his arm.

Oren rubbed his arm. "Ouch that hurt!"

Terry started laughing. "Holy shit! You two are like children. Do you act like this in front of patients, too?"

"We've never actually worked together before so hopefully we'll learn how to behave ourselves," Claire said.

"So for the first time it will be in an illegal clinic," Oren said as he finished his beer and stood up. "We need another pitcher."

"I'm switching over to wine. Beer is making me feel bloated, and we haven't even eaten any dinner yet," Claire said.

Oren looked at his watch. "Megs should be here in about a half an hour. I'm not sure if she'll fancy Falconetti's or would like to go somewhere else." All of a sudden Oren looked worried.

"What's wrong? You don't want to pay extra for my wine? I'll go with a house red then," Claire said.

"No." Oren sat back down and put his hands on his head. "Megs can't know about this."

"Shit, you're right Oren. It would break her heart."

"Well we won't tell her then," Terry said.

"We can't hide the clinic from her; it's bound to come out sooner or later," Claire said.

"No Claire. Terry's right. We can't tell her anything. You've had countless arguments about alternative medicine with her, so she'd see through our homeopathy front straight away."

Claire was nodding in agreement. "And she would visit our clinic and want to help us set it up."

"So you're saying she knows about homeopathy?" Terry asked.

"She knows more about herbal remedies and those stupid sugar pills than most homeopaths do. I can just imagine how she'd scrutinize every little detail in the clinic," Claire said.

"Claire and Megs won't even talk about homeopathy anymore. They get so wound up with each other that they go for the jugular," Oren said as he picked up the butter knife on the table and stabbed in into the air.

"You're exaggerating Oren! Look Terry. It's nothing personal with Megs, but I still can't believe someone so intelligent believes in that nonsense," Claire said.

Terry started laughing. "Those are cruel words Claire."

Oren nodded in agreement.

"To hell with both of you then!" Claire said and she slumped back into her chair.

"Come on Claire, you're being super harsh," Oren said.

"Whatever," Claire said and she signalled the waitress to come over. "I need another drink. I hate it when people gang up on me."

"Stop being such a drama queen," Oren said.

"Another pitcher?" the waitress asked.

"Sure," Oren said. "And could you bring over the wine list, too?"

"Actually I'll just have your house red," Claire said.

Claire picked up her Blackberry and started perusing the internet. Oren thought she was sulking so he just ignored her and started to talk to Terry. He hated it when she acted like that. A few minutes later the waitress came back with their drinks.

"Thanks," Claire said and she sipped her wine.

"So are you going to join us now or are you still lost in internet-land? I find that so rude when people do that," Oren said.

"For your information I've found a great alibi to get me into the States," Claire said and she slid her phone over to Oren.

"Why do you need an alibi?" Terry asked.

"I'm a terrible liar and the customs officer will see right through me and most likely search my car," Claire said.

"You'll have nothing going into the States and sugar pills coming back into Canada. It's not like you're going to be caught with coke or guns or something," Terry said.

Claire shrugged. "They'll make me pay duty and taxes. I'll definitely be over my limit."

Oren was finished reading the webpage on Claire's cell phone. "Actually, that seminar looks really interesting and perhaps even relevant." Oren handed the cell phone over to Terry who read the title of the seminar out loud. "Medical marijuana versus opiates, which is the safer option for pain management?"

"Too bad this seminar is offered in Seattle. Many doctors in Vancouver would benefit from this, too," Oren said.

Terry gave Claire her cell phone back. "I'm sure many doctors from this side of the border will be there. I'm tempted, too. I often avoid prescribing marijuana because I don't know how to measure the appropriate dosage. Methadone or fentanyl is so much easier," Terry said.

"But I've never heard of someone overdosing on marijuana. Opiates on the other hand..."

Claire was interrupted by Oren. "Let's change the subject 'cause we'll talk ourselves out of our original plan." Oren looked around and lowered his voice. "We just have to be careful how much we prescribe, even if it is anything at all. We need to consider the patient's medical history, their health, everything. If a patient overdoses on us we're busted."

Just as Claire and Terry nodded in agreement Megs walked up to their table.

"What's all this whispering about? I feel like I'm intruding." Oren got up and grabbed another chair. He took off Megs' coat and she sat down. Claire was worried that Megs heard part of their conversation. She was frustrated with how careless they were.

Terry leaned over the table and spoke in a low voice. "Sorry Megs. I just didn't want people to hear our conversation about my separation."

Megs took Terry's hand. "I'm so sorry to hear about that. If you need anything, even just to talk about it, we're here for you."

"Thanks Megs," Terry said.

"How's Ethan doing?" Megs asked.

"He's too young to really understand," Terry replied.

"That's probably a good thing," Claire said and Terry nodded.

"Oren told me that you are going to court soon. That's so awful," Megs said.

"This Thursday actually," Terry said.

"Shit man. You must be stressed," Claire said.

"Not anymore. I'm too tired to care. At the end of the day all I care about is regularly seeing Ethan."

"Do you have a good lawyer?" Claire asked.

"Claire!" Megs said and she gave Claire a stern look.

"Don't worry Megs. I actually like Claire's straightforwardness," Terry said.

Claire smiled.

"Don't we all?" Oren said as he winked at Claire.

"I apparently have one of the best lawyers this city has to offer. My babysitter's much older boyfriend who hates cheaters. So he's taking this one personally and only charging me 'mates rates' as he calls it," Terry said.

"Mates rates? Is he British or something?" Claire asked.

"Yep. And he's a super nice guy." Terry finished his beer and slammed it on the table. "Let's change the subject. I'm starving."

"Can't we just eat here?" Megs asked.

The three doctors agreed. "I do love their pizzas," Claire said.

"They also have poutine with real cheese curds," Oren said.

Claire rolled her eyes. "I'm tired of fighting with you tonight."

"Oh c'mon, Claire. You know I'm just kidding."

"What were you guys fighting about?" Megs asked.

"Just the same old shit Megs. You know how it is." Claire got up and grabbed some menus from the bar. She was getting annoyed with the lack of service, but was too hungry to wait for the server. Claire was worried that they scared the staff off. *Did they hear our conversation?* Claire thought to herself.

"Sorry about that," the bartender said. Claire looked up as she was startled from her daydream. "Sorry?" Claire asked.

"We are down one server tonight, but we have someone else coming in to replace her," the bartender added.

"Oh. No problem." Claire said and then walked back to her friends and dropped the menus on the table.

"Are you alright Claire?" Megs asked.

"I'm out of it because I'm so goddamn hungry!" Claire sat down and smiled.

Claire was convinced that none of the bar staff as well as Megs heard their conversation. She desperately wanted that feeling of paranoia to go away. She decided that alcohol on an empty stomach was probably not a good idea, and it made her feel out of sorts. So Claire decided to have one more glass of wine with her dinner and go home straight afterwards. Megs would definitely notice that something was up if Claire chose not to have a drink with her meal.

Chapter 7

It has been a number of months since the pseudo-clinic first opened; and as Claire predicted, they were quickly acquiring patients. Some legitimately wanted homeopathic treatments, but many others needed pain medication. The doctors only asked health-related questions in order to ensure that the patients were in relatively good health. The last thing they needed was one of their patients to be rushed to the hospital or worse. If this did happen, the police would surely be able to trace the prescription back to their clinic. However, Oren was more concerned with an observant pharmacist who would end up recognising that one of the doctors was overprescribing narcotics. So they kept track of where their patients lived, and which pharmacy they took their prescriptions to. These patients didn't want to lose their drug source so they were also very careful. The doctors all felt that it was a fail-safe arrangement.

"It isn't very often you see an MD working at a holistic clinic," said an elderly lady.

Claire smiled. "There are more around than you would think."

"That's the reason I chose this clinic."

"Oh okay. So Mrs. Bannis, can you tell me why you're here today?"

"Well, I've had a bellyache for a long while now."

"Can you describe your symptoms?" Claire asked.

"My belly hurts and when I do finally get a bit of an appetite, and eat, it really starts hurting even more. So I'm afraid to eat now."

"And how long has this been going on for?" Claire asked.

"A few weeks I think. Maybe a month, I don't know," Mrs. Bannis replied.

"And did you see your family doctor?"

"Yes I did. And he prescribed me these pills." Mrs. Bannis opened up her purse, took out an empty pill bottle and handed it over to Claire.

Claire looked at the bottle's label which read *pantoprazole magnesium*.

"This is a common prescription, but can you try and remember how long you have been taking these?"

Mrs. Bannis looked over to the wall. "My doctor gave me a repeat prescription five times. And I took it back to the pharmacist to have it refilled three times. But they aren't working. That's why I'm here hoping that you will give me an herbal remedy that will fix my stomach."

"Okay. This information is good," Claire said.

If indeed the symptoms persisted after taking this prescription for nearly a month, Claire was worried that Mrs. Bannis may have a stomach ulcer, but the word cancer stuck out in the back of her mind. Claire pushed that thought away and continued with her patient interview.

"So Mrs. Bannis. Why didn't you go back to see your doctor when you didn't think that these pills were working?" Claire asked.

Mrs. Bannis just shrugged her shoulders.

"Well, before I can give you any herbal remedies, we must rule out the possibility that it is a stomach ulcer." Mrs. Bannis looked at Claire without any emotion so she continued.

"If it is a stomach ulcer you need antibiotics. Are you allergic to penicillin?"

Mrs. Bannis slammed her hand on the desk which startled Claire. "I came here for something natural. I'm so sick and tired of taking those chemicals."

"But penicillin is natural, it's virtually mould," Claire said.

Mrs. Bannis' face softened. "That seems to ring a bell."

"Have you ever heard of a man called Alexander Fleming?" Claire asked.

"Why, yes I have," Mrs. Bannis said. Claire could see the recognition of his name in the old lady's face. "Well, can you give me some penicillin then?"

"No I can't." Claire reached out and grabbed Mrs. Bannis' hands. This tactic worked for her many times in the past when trying to obtain a patient's trust. A touch goes a long way.

"We need to be sure that you do not have an ulcer. You need an x-ray. I can call the hospital and set you up an appointment today."

Mrs. Bannis looked confused. "Why can't you just give me some penicillin?"

"If you take too many antibiotics, there is a chance that your body will become immune to them. So we now only prescribe antibiotics if we are certain that you need them."

Mrs. Bannis let go of Claire's hands and shrugged her shoulders. "Well, it's not like I have anything else better to do."

Claire was relieved, especially with elderly people she just didn't want to take the chance. She picked up the phone and called the radiology department in the hospital. Claire was relieved that they were able to fit Mrs. Bannis in this afternoon.

Mrs. Bannis opened up her purse and took out her cheque book. Claire's conscience overcame her. They were generating more than enough money through prescribing narcotics that losing a couple hundred dollars wasn't a big deal. "There is no need to pay for this session." Mrs. Bannis looked confused.

"The price of the consultation includes the alternative medicine that I'm not giving you. So this session is free," Claire said.

"Well thank you doctor." Mrs. Bannis put her cheque book back into her purse.

Claire helped Mrs. Bannis up from her chair and escorted her to the door. Her feeling of relief was overshadowed by the thought of what would have happened if Mrs. Bannis saw a real homeopath. Claire was certain that there was something seriously wrong with the patient. Most likely it was an ulcer, but stomach cancer was a definitely possibility too. But then again, what the hell was her family doctor thinking? Claire decided that there were too many unknowns to criticize anybody.

Claire's thoughts were interrupted by Terry's entry into the clinic. He was taking over for Claire who wanted to keep her shifts at the walk-in clinic. She considered the pseudo-clinic a temporary measure, and she didn't want to lose her position at her real clinic. However, she was more than happy to get rid of her hospital shifts. The money was pretty good, especially when she delivered babies in the middle of the night; but what they were making at their pseudo-clinic was crazy. Some days they would make over $10,000. Sure, it was split among the three doctors, but it was tax-free. Claire was already putting a big dent in her car loan. Her student loan was low interest, so it was not much of a priority. It was not like her car loan. For the first time since Claire started university, she started to see the light at the end of the financial tunnel.

*****

Oren was in the second treatment room seeing a patient who was in her mid-30s. She seemed to be a bit on the edge but Oren had a natural ability to calm people down, especially women. "Are you okay?" Oren asked.

The woman couldn't even make eye contact with Oren. "I've never done anything like this before. So yeah, I'm a bit nervous."

"There's nothing to be worried about. If someone asks what you were doing in here, tell them you were getting some herbal remedies for anxiety or stress. St. John's Wart is a popular one." The woman took a deep breath, which seemed to relax her. She looked over to Oren and nodded.

"How did you find out about us?" Oren asked.

"My brother, you gave him a much-needed prescription for Vicodin. He's in a lot of pain and most doctors don't give a shit."

Oren would be able to check back in the records in order to determine which patients were prescribed Vicodin and the reason why, so he didn't prod further.

"And what about you? What can I do for you?" Oren asked.

"I need Valium."

"Can you tell me why?"

The patient looked around the room possibly to avoid eye contact with Oren. "I'm flying out to see my sister in a couple of days and I'm super scared."

"You're afraid of flying?"

"Absolutely, I'm terrified of flying."

Oren suspected that the patient was lying, but he didn't care. He considered Valium to be relatively safe, unless it was mixed with something else.

"Before I give you a prescription I need to ask you a few questions."

The patient nodded.

"Have you ever taken Valium before?"

"Yes, every time I fly."

"And how often is that?"

"A couple times per year."

"Do you drink?"

The patient gave Oren a dirty look, but answered his question anyways.

"Yes, but only occasionally."

Oren suspected that that answer was a lie. However, most patients lie about how much they drink. Oren normally doubled the units in order to get a more accurate picture of his patient's drinking habit.

"I didn't mean to offend you. It is a question that I must ask everyone. It is very dangerous to mix alcohol and diazepam."

"Diazepam?" the patient asked.

"Diazepam is the same thing. It's no longer marketed as Valium."

The patient didn't say anything.

"Okay. Let's continue." Oren looked down at his checklist. "Is there a chance that you are pregnant?"

"No."

"Now I need you to think back to when you were taking Valium in the past."

The patient stared back at Oren. She seemed much calmer than when she first sat down in the treatment room.

"Did you ever feel dizzy?"

"No."

"Did you ever feel nauseous?"

"No."

Oren kept going through the checklist, but he felt that it was a pointless exercise. The patient was just going to lie in order to get her much-needed prescription.

"We're nearly done here, but I do have one more question. Why didn't you ask your doctor to prescribe you Valium? I mean, it's quite common for doctors to prescribe Valium to patients who are afraid of flying."

"He won't prescribe them to me anymore," the patient said.

And the plot thickened. Oren was certain that she was addicted. A part of him didn't want to prescribe her diazepam, but his ethics went out the window when they first opened the fake clinic. And of course these people, these desperate people, were the ones they made money from. So as Oren did many times per day, he wrote another prescription, this time for diazepam and gave it to the patient. He knew he'd see her again. Returning customers were ideal, and they were the ones who kept the clinic running. He needed to safely feed their addiction.

The patient put the prescription in her purse, and pulled out some cash and handed it to Oren.

Neither Oren nor the patient said good-bye. She just headed straight to the door and sheepishly slipped out of the building without looking at anyone.

After she left, Oren went out into the waiting room and called another patient in. Oren was quite thankful that this patient didn't look like a granola-eating hippie as he hated going through the homeopathic bullshit. Although he agreed with Claire and Terry that the holistic front was necessary, he felt that it was also an utter waste of time. What they generated off of the homeopathic crap was peanuts compared to the prescriptions. And Oren was sure that this young and dopey-looking punk who was slouched in his chair and glued to his cell phone wanted some narcotics, which he was more than happy to prescribe.

Chapter 8

The sea was calm and the sun was shining, it was a glorious day. Claire and five other divers were heading out on a boat to a beautiful reef in the Caribbean. She didn't know anybody as she decided to go on holiday by herself. Claire was super stressed at work with the fake clinic and the constant paranoia, so she decided to take a much-needed break. This was the first time she ever went on holiday on her own.

The boat finally stopped and everyone started to put on their diving gear. Claire zipped up her wetsuit, put on her goggles and fins. The diving instructor walked over to Claire and helped her with her tanks. Claire sat on the side of the boat and put the regulator in her mouth, and pulled the goggles over her eyes. She then fell backwards off the side of the boat into the beautiful warm waters. Claire, with the rest of the divers, held their arms up over their head letting the air out of their vests; and they slowly sank towards the reef below them.

Claire was partnered up with one of the divers who she only met that morning. She kept him in sight as she swam around the reef. The colours of the fish were phenomenal. A school of fish surrounded her, nibbling at her legs. She laughed into her regulator and then the fish finally swam away. Claire then saw a sea turtle, she was certain that it was a hawksbill. She followed it for a bit but it quickly out-swam her. Then in the corner of her eye she saw something glowing red. She immediately turned towards it and its shape was similar to that of a stingray. She carefully swam towards it. The ray must have sensed that Claire was approaching, so it also started to move away; and as it did it started to glow a bright red. Claire thought her eyes were playing tricks on her. She continued to follow it hoping to get a closer look. The stingray started to descend deeper into the sea and Claire continued to follow it. She began to feel uncomfortable with the depth that she was going and tried to stop, but she couldn't. Claire couldn't tear her eyes away from the radiant red colour emanating from the stingray. Her mind was telling her to turn around and swim back to the surface; but her body could not as if she were tethered to the stingray. Claire started to panic as she knew she was far too deep, but she still couldn't get her body to stop following the stingray. Claire's mind was going crazy as she descended into the dark depths of the ocean, but the more she panicked the faster she swam towards the glowing red sting ray. Claire's head started to feel as if it were being crushed. She could see blood on her goggles and she knew it was coming from her eyes. She started screaming. All of a sudden she started to hear some music. The lyrics were getting louder and louder.

"We get these pills to swallow"
"How they stick"
"In your throat"
"Taste like gold"

Claire's eyes opened staring directly at her clock. It was 10:30 a.m. She picked up her cell and saw that it was Oren. Still shaken up from her dream, she answered her phone.

"You better not be asking me to come in today. It's my day off," Claire said.

"Normal people say hello when they answer the phone," Oren said.

"Fuck you," Claire said.

Oren laughed. "Did somebody wake up on the wrong side of the bed?"

"Actually, I'm really happy that you called. You saved me from drowning," Claire said.

"What?" Oren asked.

"Nevermind. It was just a nightmare," Claire said.

"That's good. I thought you'd be pissed off because I called you before noon on your day off, but I really need to talk to you."

Claire could hear a hint of excitement in Oren's voice.

"Now?" Claire asked.

"After my shift this afternoon. Will you be home?"

"Yeah. It sounds like you have some good news."

"Just you wait. I have to get back to work now," Oren said.

Claire and Oren said their good-byes and hung up.

Claire could feel the man stir next to her. She couldn't remember his name. Was it Frank, Franco or François? It was something like that and he certainly was cute. She could barely remember the night before. Last night she went out with some friends, including Megs, and got completely wasted. Claire started to run her hands through his dark brown hair and he opened his eyes and smiled. She moved closer and they started to kiss. Just when things started to heat up again the man leaned over top of Claire and grabbed a little make-up mirror and a rolled up $20 bill and placed them on her stomach. Memories from the night before started to flood Claire's mind. There was a bit of coke remaining, so the man made a couple of lines on the mirror. He snorted one and then Claire sat up. She leaned over and snorted the remaining line. The man started to kiss Claire again first on her lips and then on her neck. Claire started to remember how amazing the man was in bed. He moved to her breasts and then to her stomach. The coke started to kick in and Claire felt amazing. With his lips barely touching Claire's skin, he moved down her body and started to kiss her outer thighs and then her inner thighs. Claire's breath deepened and she started to gently pull the man's hair. She looked up at the ceiling, and then closed her eyes. Any remnants of her nightmare were completely forgotten. She closed her eyes and enjoyed the man's tongue between her legs.

*****

It was late in the afternoon and Claire was starting to get annoyed with Oren, who still hadn't shown up. She tried calling his cell numerous times, but it went directly to his voice mail. It's not like she had any plans, but she couldn't exactly go anywhere either. After the man left her apartment she felt so empty and alone. Initially, she was confused why she felt that way about someone she only knew for 12 hours, but eventually recognised it as part of a come down from hours of excessive cocaine use. She was also feeling really irritated especially towards Oren and his tardiness, but decided to keep that under control when and if he would eventually arrive. Oren may pick up on her being out of character. She was sure that he'd seen the coke in her purse the night of the party many months ago. Claire started to get angry with the thought of Oren snatching her purse from her hands and sifting around finding Mallory Nixon's Valium. What an asshole! Claire stopped that thought in its tracks. She was doing it again for the 20th time that day, which was getting overly pissed off at something that happened in the past. "Fucking coke," Claire said to herself.

There was a knock at the door, and Oren tried turning the knob but it was locked. Claire went over to the door and let him in.

Straight away Oren went down on one knee and opened up a box with a dazzling diamond ring. "Megan Maria Jiménez Jones, will you marry me?" Oren asked.

Claire initially looked shocked and then joined him on the floor and gave him a big hug.

"Oh my god! That's awesome!" Claire said.

"So I get your approval then?"

"Megs is going to go nuts," Claire said.

"Good nuts or bad nuts?" Oren asked.

"She's so going to cry." Claire said.

"Happy tears?" Oren asked.

"Oh stop being so damn stupid, of course she's going to be happy!" Claire said.

Oren helped Claire up and they walked over to the couch.

"We need some wine to celebrate," Claire said.

"Okay. Just one glass to help calm my nerves. We're going out for dinner tonight at the Sandbar and I was going to ask her there."

"At the restaurant?" Claire asked.

"Well, yeah," Oren replied.

"Don't ask her at the restaurant. Trust me on this one Oren. You know how she is when it comes to being the centre of attention. She'd be put on the spotlight in public," Claire said.

"Yeah, you're right. Then where do you suggest?"

"You'll be on Granville Island so after supper take her outside by the water facing downtown. Ask her then," Claire said.

"Before supper?"

Claire crossed her arms. "Why are men so dumb?"

Oren just shrugged.

"After she says yes, all you two will want to do is go home and screw so it's best to eat first."

Oren started laughing. "Claire, you speak with such elegance."

"Sorry. You and Megs will want to make passionate love all through the night."

"That's more like it," Oren said.

"And make sure you go down on her, too. The guy that I had here a few hours ago was amazing at that. He took me to heaven and..."

Oren interrupted Claire. "Okay. Enough! That's way too much information."

Claire laughed as she knew that Oren hated it when she talked about her sexual relations. She went into the kitchen and brought out two glasses of red for her and Oren.

"This smells like a Rioja," Oren said.

"Campo Viejo. It's nothing special, but it's the most expensive one that I have in my nearly empty wine rack," Claire said.

"Claire, I recall your wine rack being pretty much full a few weeks ago."

Claire shrugged her shoulders. "So I'm a wino."

Claire sat down beside Oren and held up her glass. "To you and Megs."

They cheered each other and took a sip of their wine.

"I'm so nervous Claire," Oren said.

"You'll be fine. She's going to say yes," Claire said.

"Are you sure?" Oren asked.

Claire looked directly into Oren's eyes. "Yes. Now calm down."

Oren leaned over and kissed Claire on her cheek. "Thanks for your support."

Claire started to feel uncomfortable because she didn't like to deal with emotional stuff for too long, so she quickly tried to change the subject. "So I guess you won't be in tomorrow."

"No way. And Megs took the day off, too. It's our anniversary."

"Oh my god. I completely forgot!" Claire said.

"It's crazy how fast the years are going by. It seems like yesterday when you set us up."

Claire didn't want to go the emotional route again so she tried to steer away from it.

"I never set you up. You just happened to be at the same party."

Claire never saw him so giddy before and she preferred dealing with the more level-headed Oren. Although, he was right, she totally set them up.

"So what made you to finally decide to ask for her hand in marriage?" Claire asked in a goofy voice.

"I don't know. It just felt right." Oren paused for a few seconds. "Perhaps it's because for the first time in my entire life I'm debt-free."

Claire looked confused.

"I feel so free Claire. Financially free."

Claire understood as she was feeling the same way. With all the extra money she was earning at the homeopathy clinic, she had nearly paid off her debts. And she still had enough to spend it on partying almost every week.

Oren looked at his watch and finished his glass of wine. "I have to go. Our reservations are for 8 tonight."

Claire got up and escorted Oren to the door. They hugged and he left. Claire sat back down on the couch once again feeling utterly alone. She felt so hollow, so empty. She poured another glass of wine and turned on the TV. The only half decent thing that was on was Dexter. *That will do* Claire thought and she wrapped a blanket tightly around her body. She knew what would make her happy again, but she didn't want to fall down the rabbit hole. Claire loved that cliché and oddly enough it kept her in check as she pictured herself jumping into a dark abyss feet first and landing in a lake of fire. She didn't believe in heaven or hell or even God for that matter, but she believed in death. She treated many patients who were struggling with drug addiction that it was enough to put any sane person off. So she persevered through her come down hoping that Dexter would keep her mind occupied until that awful feeling would go away. Claire asked herself. "Is it really worth it?" Maybe not now but it will be the next time she's out partying. She'll forget this whole ordeal as she has done many times before.

Chapter 9

As Claire was writing out a prescription on her desk for oxycodone she was startled by her patient's abrupt movement as he grabbed something from behind his back. Claire looked up and her whole body froze. *This is it* she thought. *He's going to cuff me. I'm going to jail.*

The patient looked confused. "Here's your money." And he took a stack of bills out of his wallet and placed them on her desk.

Claire quickly looked down and finished writing out the prescription. Claire was not relieved. She remembered that they would have to complete the transaction first before he could make the arrest. Claire pushed the prescription towards the patient and he picked it up and put it in his wallet. "Thanks. See you in a few weeks." And the patient left the treatment room shutting the door behind him.

Claire sat at her desk motionless for a few minutes waiting for the bust, but it never came. Then Claire recalled that he said he'll come back, and so she guessed he would become a regular customer at the clinic. Claire's mind started to race and she began to think that perhaps he was an undercover cop trying to compile a strong case against the clinic. "Stupid paranoia," Claire whispered to herself and she took a couple of blue pills that she kept in her purse. Claire closed her eyes and let the Valium work its way through her body.

There was a knock at the door and Terry popped his head into the treatment room.

"Hey Claire. Are you going to the party tonight?"

Claire quickly snapped back into reality. "I have no choice, I'm a bridesmaid."

"Well aren't you a bag of joy today," Terry said.

"Well who the hell has engagement parties nowadays?" Claire asked.

"Lots of people," Terry replied.

Claire rolled her eyes. "Whatever."

"Jesus Claire, someone needs to take a happy pill."

Claire could barely keep a neutral face since she just took two happy pills. "You know I'm just kidding around, of course I'm excited. I would have been her Maid of Honour if it wasn't for her little sister."

"I'll never understand your humour Claire. See you tonight," Terry said and he closed the door leaving Claire alone in the treatment room.

As Terry was about to leave the clinic he noticed a man sitting quietly in the waiting room.

"Can I help you?" Terry asked.

The man looked up from reading his newspaper and removed his glasses.

"I'm here to see Dr. O'Brian."

Terry couldn't exactly pinpoint his accent. "He's busy with a patient right now, but Dr. Lalonde is currently free."

The man smiled and put his glasses back on. "I'll wait." And he started to read the newspaper again.

Something didn't seem right about this man. Terry couldn't imagine him as an advocate of homeopathy. And he didn't look like the type who'd be into narcotics, either. Perhaps it was just the way he dressed. His suit looked very expensive. Then the word "cop" popped into Terry's head. He couldn't risk it, so he had to get out of the clinic immediately. Should he warn the others? What if he's wrong? The man glanced over his newspaper and looked at Terry. *Shit.* Terry thought. *I'm staring at him.*

"Okay. I will let Dr. O'Brian know." Terry walked over to one of the treatment rooms and knocked on the door.

When Oren opened the door he could see that Terry looked worried. "Sorry to bother you Oren, but you have a patient who is waiting to see you." Oren looked over Terry's shoulder and clocked the situation straight away.

"Thanks for letting me know. Shouldn't you be done for the day?" Terry nodded in agreement and left the clinic.

Oren was nearly finished with his legitimate patient who wanted something herbal to boost her sex drive. He gave her some magic sugar pills and a list of foods that would raise her libido. He thought that she'd be better off with a good vibrator and some erotica novels, but bit his tongue. If this placebo worked she would come back again, and maybe even tell her friends about the clinic. That's how their recognition was spreading, through word of mouth. The clinic was pretty much busy every day and the money was rolling in.

Oren led the patient out of the treatment room, and as he was saying good-bye he was discretely analysing the man. He was in his mid-50s, greying hair and well-dressed. Terry was right, this was an undercover cop, but Oren wasn't nervous. He just finished seeing a real patient and he had the notes to prove it, which were still on his desk. He planned to deny everything.

"Can I help you?" Oren asked.

The man folded his newspaper and he picked up his briefcase.

"Can we have a chat?" the man asked.

"Sure," Oren said.

"Privately," the man said.

So Oren led the way to the empty treatment room.

The man took a seat and crossed his legs. And that was when Oren started to get nervous. He closed the door and sat down at his desk.

"So how can I help you?" Oren asked.

"Well Doctor, I have a few questions for you."

"How about a name first? You seem to already know me."

"Doug. Just call me Doug."

Oren finally pinpointed his unfamiliar accent. The man was South African.

"Okay Doug. What are your questions?" Oren started to get annoyed with this cop and he wanted him to get straight to the point.

Doug put his briefcase on his lap and opened it up.

The first thing that came to Oren's mind was that Doug was going to produce a warrant for his arrest. Instead, he started to pull out empty pill bottles from his briefcase and he placed them on the desk. He lined up eight all together in a neat row. Oren was confused so he picked up a bottle and read the prescription. It was oxycodone, which was prescribed by him. He picked up another bottle and it, too, was a narcotic prescribed by him. All of the bottles were.

"How did you get these?" Oren asked.

"I'm asking the questions," Doug said and he closed his briefcase and placed it on the floor.

Cop or not, Oren didn't like the way Doug was talking to him. "Well then ask them. And stop wasting my goddamn time."

"I also have pill bottle samples with Dr. Lalonde and Dr. Wu's names on them, but from what I can gather you're the ring leader of this gong show."

Oren stood up as he had enough. "I think we're done here."

Doug grabbed a photo from the inside of his suit pocket and threw it on the desk. Oren looked down and he started to feel nauseous. The photo was the dopey-looking punk who was one of Oren's regular customers. He was tied up and his face was beaten pretty badly. Upon closer inspection Oren saw that his throat was slit and the kid was dead. He pushed the photo back towards Doug and slowly sat back down again.

"You're not a cop. You're a goddamn drug dealer."

Doug started laughing. "You thought I was a cop?"

Oren didn't say a word as he was both scared and angry.

"The kid deserved to die. He was selling drugs on my turf. And he was warned. That's what happens if you don't listen to me."

"What do you want from me?" Oren asked.

"Don't worry. I'm not here to kill you. I'm actually intrigued with your little set up here. I mean, no one would ever suspect a doctor to be a drug dealer."

Doug picked up the previous patient's medical sheet that was left on the desk. "And this homeopathy front. Such a clever idea. I bet it was the lady doctor's idea."

Oren started to wonder how much Doug knew about the clinic. He must have been doing his own investigation for a while now and most likely he had his thugs doing the groundwork. They were probably coming in disguised as patients.

"Look. I didn't know that my patients would sell their drugs on the street. I thought it was for them. For their personal use," Oren said.

"I figured that. You are very naive Doctor," Doug said.

Oren started to feel sick again and he wondered when this confrontation would end.

"Your naivety has landed you in hot water with me, but I have a proposal." Doug sat up and leaned on the desk. "I have a shipment of morphine scheduled to come in next week and I need to move it quickly."

Oren knew that this wasn't a proposal whereby he'd have the choice to accept it or not. So he sat very still and continued to listen to Doug.

"And I'm going to sell it through your clinic."

Oren shuddered at that thought.

"Do I make you feel uncomfortable?"

Oren nodded.

"I'm not asking you to buy my morphine. There is no way you would have that kind of money. I just need to store it here and I kindly ask you to sell it on my behalf. I will send some people here to buy large quantities from you, but I also encourage you to sell it to some of your own customers as well. I mean pain medication is pain medication." Doug sat back up and crossed his legs and waited for Oren to respond.

"Why can't you just get your street goons to do this?" Oren asked.

Doug smirked and looked at the empty prescription bottles on the desk. "You know the answer to that."

"Look. I know I don't have much of a choice here, but I refuse to sell any street drugs," Oren said.

"Don't worry Doctor; my so-called goons are quite good at that. I just want to get in on the fun at your lovely homeopathy clinic."

"Are we almost done here?" Oren asked.

"Aren't you going to ask about money? You're going to make much more on my morphine than your little prescription business."

"What's my cut then?" Oren asked.

"Twenty percent. And I have millions of dollars' worth of morphine that I want you to help me sell. So do the math," Doug said.

"I don't even know how much morphine goes for on the street," Oren said.

Doug grabbed the prescription pad that was on the desk and he wrote all the monetary details down.

"It's pretty straightforward. We'll collect the money once per week. And if what you sold and what you give us doesn't add up." Doug started tapping his finger next to the picture of Oren's dead customer on the desk. "And I expect the entire shipment to sell in a month." Doug got up and grabbed his briefcase. "I'll be in touch." And Doug left the clinic.

Within seconds of Doug leaving the clinic, Claire busted into the treatment room. "Holy evil, pale blue eyes! Was that a cop or something?" Oren was hunched over vomiting into the garbage can.

"Shit Oren." Claire ran over and started to rub his back. She could tell that something was wrong. "Are we busted?"

Oren slowly sat up and wiped his mouth. "Worse."

Claire looked confused. "What could be worse than a cop?"

"A drug dealer. Actually, not just a drug dealer but some big drug lord. Fuck, I don't know. But he killed one of my patients for selling my prescription drugs on his turf."

Claire noticed the picture on the desk and she got up and quickly left the room. When she returned she had an empty garbage can and threw it on the floor. She then picked up the photo trying not to look at it too closely and set it on fire, throwing it into the garbage can.

"You're going to set the fire alarm off Claire."

Oren was right, so Claire took the garbage can outside to the back alley and waited for it to finish burning. When she returned she locked the clinic door and drew the blinds.

"Okay. What the hell is going on Oren? I'm shitting in my pants right now."

"We have to sell his morphine. He's going to bring it in next week," Oren said.

"How much morphine?" Claire asked.

Oren handed the paper with Doug's monetary details to Claire.

"Twenty percent, eh?" Claire said.

"It's a lot and I'll split it three ways," Oren said.

"You know that this is just the beginning. This won't be a one-time thing," Claire said.

"I know," Oren said.

"Should we really be involving Terry with this?" Claire asked.

"And how are we going to hide it from him, Claire? Tell him that he can no longer go into the storage room?"

"We should give him the option to get out then," Claire said.

"You're right. For the sake of his son," Oren said.

"But what if he tells his lawyer or the police?" Claire asked.

"If Terry did that all three of us would be dead," Oren replied.

"Jesus," Claire said.

"I don't even want you involved," Oren said.

"I'm not leaving you alone to deal with this shit. Plus, it's a lot of money," Claire said.

Oren knew that he would not be able to talk Claire out of it. She was one of the most stubborn people he knew, besides himself.

"My engagement party is tonight," Oren said and he put his head in his hands.

Claire started to rub Oren's back again. "Let's close the clinic early today. Megs is home stressing out about the party tonight and she could use some moral support."

Oren stood up and looked at Claire. "You're right. Is it okay if you close shop? I need to get out of here."

Claire nodded and Oren quickly left the clinic. She locked the door behind Oren and went straight to her purse to take some more Valium. She was running low and decided that she would soon have to write a prescription out for herself. She had mastered copying Oren's signature. And after today she would need much more to calm her nerves.

*****

"Aren't you hungry Oren? We spent a fortune on these hors d'oeuvres and I haven't even seen you take a bite," Megs said.

Oren took Megs hands and kissed her fingertips. "Thanks for organizing this. I've just been carried away in conversations that I forgot to eat."

In reality Oren had no appetite, and he couldn't stop thinking about his earlier confrontation with Doug. The thought of food made him feel nauseous.

"Look at these two lovebirds." One of Megs' friends came over and hugged her and Oren. "Congratulations. Did you set a date yet?"

"Not yet. We have to save some money first. Maybe in a year or so," Megs said.

Oren couldn't help but think that he'd be able to cover the cost of the wedding after one month working for Doug.

"Wow. What a rock!" Megs' friend, who Oren found slightly irritating, was gawking over the engagement ring, which was the theme of the night.

"Aren't you a lucky girl?"

Oren couldn't take it anymore. He started to look around for Claire and found her mingling with a group of their colleagues, including Terry. She looked so relaxed, which pissed Oren off. He couldn't understand how she could act so natural and happy after what they went through earlier that day.

"Hey man, congratulations." Oren's colleagues were shaking his hand and giving him hugs, and he entertained them with some small talk for a few minutes.

Oren leaned towards Claire and asked to see her privately and she followed him out to the lobby of the hotel.

"This place must have cost you a pretty penny to rent. Wouldn't it have been more economical to have your party at home?" Oren ignored Claire's taunts and walked right out of the front doors.

Claire chased after him. "Where the hell are you going Oren?"

Claire finally caught up to Oren, who eventually stopped and sat down on a bench in the hotel gardens. Claire sat down next to him.

"You want to talk about this afternoon. Don't you?" Claire said.

Oren shook his head. "No, I want whatever you had that made you look so goddamn relaxed and happy. There's no way that you're doing this on your own."

"I've had some Valium. Do you want some?"

"You have something else in your purse Claire, and it's not Valium. I've been immune to that shit for years."

"I didn't know you were a pill popper."

"I was after my mother died. My father was on loads of drugs for depression and I used to steal them. He must have known, but he never said a word. I guess I was easier to handle when I was on them."

"You were like 14 or 15," Claire said.

Oren shrugged his shoulders.

"I know that you saw my coke stash the night that you snatched my bag," Claire said.

"Yeah. Sorry about that," Oren said.

"I thought you were anti-coke," Claire said.

"I actually thought you hated that shit due to all the social and environmental issues associated with it in developing countries," Oren said.

Claire started laughing "No. That's Megs."

"We both assumed incorrectly I guess. Megs certainly has influenced us," Oren said.

"And that's why we love her," Claire said.

Claire reached in her bag and took out her coke stash. And to Oren's surprise she removed a small spoon hidden in her bra. "I can't have this in my clutch. It doesn't fit in my secret pocket. If Megs found it she'd never forgive me."

"Then we better keep this a secret," Oren said and he snorted a bit of coke. Claire followed suit, and they both stared up in the clear night's sky for a few minutes. Finally, Oren broke the silence. "We better go back in before we're missed. I feel so much better now. Thanks for that."

Claire and Oren stood up from the bench and walked back to the hotel.

"I have to piss," Claire said and she veered off into the lobby washroom. Oren headed straight in and saw Megs talking with some of their friends. As if on cue Stairway to Heaven started playing, so Oren walked over to Megs and pulled her onto the dance floor.

"Are you serious Oren?" Megs said.

"C'mon… We barely spoke all night. I want to dance with you," Oren said.

"It's not the fact that you want to dance, it's what you want to dance to," Megs said.

"But you love Led Zeppelin," Oren said.

"Dancing to Stairway to Heaven is so cliché," Megs said.

"But it's such a beautiful song and I want this dance with my beautiful lady," Oren said.

Megs gave up and put her arms around him. To her relief more people joined them on the dance floor after a couple of minutes. She felt like she was at her high school dance again.

"Babe," Megs said.

Oren who seemed to be lost in his thoughts looked down at her and smiled.

"You know that I have to go to Colombia this summer, right?" Megs said.

Oren nodded as this wasn't new to him. She would go every year to inspect the farms where she bought her flowers from to ensure that they were ethical and sustainable. Sometimes she would even find new partnerships with other flower farms.

"Well, I want you to come with me this year," Megs said.

Oren didn't expect that. "Why?"

"Because I want you to see what I do. We're getting married for god sakes and I think it's important that you know and understand my business," Megs said.

Oren started to worry about the Colombian heat. "Hanging out near the equator in the middle of the summer just doesn't appeal to me. Why not in the winter when I desperately need some Vitamin D?"

"With the Christmas Holidays and Valentine's Day all bunched up, it's a silly time for me to go." Megs stopped dancing and looked straight into Oren's eyes. "I need to go in the summer and it's already set up with the farmers, so I can't change the date anyways. Please come with me."

Oren couldn't say no, so he hugged Megs close to him and started to dance again. "Of course I'll come."

Megs was super happy. "Great. You need to take three weeks off."

"What?" Oren was thinking two weeks.

"Consider yourself lucky, before we started dating I would leave for a month at a time," Megs said.

Oren knew that he couldn't negotiate himself out of this and he was actually looking forward to travelling to a somewhat dangerous and exciting country with Megs. Perhaps he could add to her protection, although she always claimed how safe it was. They've been together for quite a few years and only once did they go on holiday, and it was for one week at a resort in Cuba. Both Oren and Megs did their backpacking across sketchy countries on their own. Oren would often travel to sub-Sahara Africa and he even volunteered with Médecins Sans Frontières in Rwanda for a year. Megs, on the other hand, spent much of her spare time in South America. She was a fluent Spanish speaker thanks to her Puerto Rican mother, so it seemed to be a logical choice.

As Stairway to Heaven was nearing its end Oren whispered into Megs' ear. "I better brush up on my Spanish, eh?" Megs laughed and squeezed him tight. Oren was on a high and he felt that nothing could bring him down. Not even Doug.

Chapter 10

Oren was sitting in the office going through some papers. He recently decided to quit his position at the walk-in clinic, and was now able to find time to catch up on filing and other managerial work at his much more financially thriving clinic.

"Hey Oren," Terry said as he opened the door.

Oren looked up. "Yeah."

"Why is the storage door locked? I need to get some more of those sugar pills," Terry said.

Oren was confused. He got up and walked to the storage room and to his surprise there was a brand-new lock on the door. Oren's heart sank. He had a difficult time finding the perfect moment to tell Terry about the morphine, so after not hearing from Doug for nearly a month he thought that the shipment would never come and that the deal was broken. Both he and Claire didn't think it was worth worrying Terry for no reason so they kept it to themselves.

Oren frantically tried to open the door but just as Terry said, it was locked. Oren ran back to his office and started to go through his desk. Terry followed him. "What the hell is going on?"

"The key must be here somewhere," Oren said. He started to throw the papers that he just filed away all over the floor. Oren couldn't find anything and slumped into his chair. His eyes then focussed on the word "doctor" written in capital letters on a manila envelope sitting on his desk. It was right under his nose all morning, but he was too involved with his paperwork to notice. Terry picked up on what Oren was staring at. "It's in there?"

"Probably," Oren said.

Oren grabbed the envelope and looked inside. Oren first took out the key and placed it on the table. He then took out a paper with what appeared to be a safe combination scribbled on it. Oren put the contents back into the envelope and walked to the storage room and Terry followed behind.

Oren was apprehensive and wished that Terry wasn't at his heels. He had no clue how much morphine would be in there and that was assuming Doug stuck with the original plan. Oren wondered what else would be in there. A gunman? Attack dogs? He knew was being paranoid but either way, he carefully unlocked the door and turned the handle. He turned on the lights and there lying on the floor were 10 large boxes.

"What's in them?" Terry asked as he approached the boxes.

"Morphine I think," Oren said.

Terry was irritated. "You knew about this?"

"No. Well, yes," Oren said.

"Jesus, Oren."

"Can we talk about this out there? Let's close the clinic for a bit. It's never that busy on Monday mornings anyways."

Terry gave a stern look to Oren and walked out of the room. He was trying really hard to contain his anger.

A few minutes later, after Oren locked the clinic's door and closed the blinds, he found Terry packing his files into boxes. "I don't want to be part of this Oren."

"I don't blame you, but please hear me out. This isn't my fault."

"It's not your fault that we are working for drug dealers?" Terry was furious. He hated when people blamed others for their bad decisions. "It's Claire's fault then? Does she know about this?" Terry started pacing back and forth in the office. "You're going to have us all killed Oren. You do realise that there are no happy endings when dealing with the drug cartel?"

Oren shook his head. "No. It's all of our faults for starting this clinic in the first place. We were so naive Terry. They have your name, too. We're in this together."

81

"What do you mean they have my name?"

"All three of us were selling prescriptions to small-time, punk-ass wannabe drug dealers who were doing it on the wrong turf." Oren raised his voice. "They even killed one of my patients, took a photo of his dead body and threatened me with it."

Terry didn't say a word. His anger turned into fear and he started to think about this son.

"Remember the guy who you thought was an undercover cop?" Oren asked.

"You told me he needed some pills for his wife." Terry looked up at Oren. "Why did you lie?"

"Both Claire and I wanted to protect you. Actually, we wanted to protect your son. And when we didn't hear from Doug for a few weeks, we hoped the problem just went away."

"His name is Doug?" Terry said.

"His first name is all I know and it's probably a pseudonym anyways. And he'll have his goons come in here to buy the morphine. He also wants us to sell it to our patients. We have a month to get rid of it," Oren said.

"Watch what you say. He may have this place bugged," Terry said.

"You think? That seems a bit too James Bond like," Oren said.

"Jesus, Oren. He broke into our storage room in the middle of the night, smuggled in the morphine and changed the locks."

Terry had a good point, which made Oren even more anxious. "How do we get out of this mess?"

Terry wished that Oren would stop being so vocal just in case their office was bugged. "Unless you want to end up like your dead patient, we must sell his drugs within the month."

82

Terry grabbed a paper and pen from the desk, wrote "bugged" on it and held it up.

Oren nodded and grabbed the paper and wrote. "After work at Claire's." Terry shook his head and wrote. "They know who we are." Oren started to feel nauseous. Terry's son isn't the only innocent who was inadvertently a part of this mess. Megs was too. Could their homes be bugged as well?

As Oren was lost in his thoughts Terry wrote "Falconetti's" on the piece of paper.

Oren nodded in agreement. He would call Claire later from a pay phone as he didn't trust his cell. Oren was actually quite relieved that she was working at the walk-in clinic all day. He didn't know how Claire would have handled the events that unfolded this morning.

*****

Terry and Oren ended up closing the clinic early and going straight to Falconetti's. They just couldn't concentrate, and so much needed to be discussed. Claire was supposed to meet them straight after her shift at the walk-in clinic, but she was already nearly 45 minutes late.

Terry kept looking at his watch. "Seriously Oren. This is getting ridiculous."

"You know how those clinics are. She'll be here soon," Oren said.

"If she isn't here by the time I'm finished my drink, I'm leaving," Terry said.

And is if she were on cue, Claire walked into the bar with a baseball cap on and giant sunglasses covering most of her face.

Oren tried hard to keep in his laughter. "Jackie Kennedy meets a disappointed Montreal Canadiens fan."

Claire didn't say a word as she sat down at the table and removed her sunglasses.

"You know I needed a bit of comic relief; so thanks for that Claire."

"This isn't the time to be an asshole Oren. I was afraid that I'd be followed."

"Did you drive here in your fancy BMW?"

"No. And please stop being a jerk. Let's just get down to business."

Oren realised that he may have gone too far. It was clear that Claire was on edge.

Oren's face became sombre. "Well, as you know, we have a shit load of morphine in our storage room that we must sell within a month. And Terry and I were trying to think of ways out of this mess but we're stumped."

Oren stopped talking as he noticed the waitress was coming over.

"Would you like a drink?"

"A glass of your house red," Claire replied.

"Are you boys okay?" the waitress asked.

And both Terry and Oren nodded yes and smiled.

After the waitress was out of earshot, Claire jumped into the conversation. "We have no other choice but to sell the morphine. God only knows what Doug would do to us if we refuse to comply."

"What about going to the cops?" Terry asked.

"I don't want to risk it. They may find out about our illegal prescriptions." Claire abruptly stopped talking as the waitress approached their table with her glass of wine.

"Thank you," Claire said.

She took a big sip of her wine as if she was drinking water and continued. "And if we go to the cops Doug may kill us."

Oren nodded in agreement. "I think I'm with Claire on this Terry. It seems easier just to sell the goddamn morphine."

"I know. I'm just trying to lay out all of our options. I'm just afraid that the morphine is only the beginning. Who knows what he'll make us sell the next time around," Terry said.

"And that's assuming there will be a next time around," Claire said.

"Unfortunately, I think Terry is right Claire. This may only be the beginning."

"Oh for fuck sakes." And Claire downed the rest of her wine.

"Look. I've already been here for two hours and I want to go home. So what's the consensus?" Terry asked.

"The safest option is to sell the morphine," Claire said.

"Do you agree with that Terry?" Oren asked.

Terry clenched his fists and closed his eyes. "Yes," he finally replied.

Chapter 11

It was the first day that Claire was working since the morphine appeared in the storage room. The meeting at Falconetti's a few nights ago just made her more nervous, as she never saw Oren so uncertain and scared before. And to Claire that meant they were all fucked. She felt like a bird stuck in a cage, yet it had no bars. She could just drop everything and run. But where would that leave Oren and Terry? Or even Megs for that matter. Claire couldn't handle those thoughts anymore, so she grabbed her purse and took some more Valium.

Meanwhile, in the other treatment room, Oren was staring at a large blue sports bags that was placed on his desk. An unassuming man of medium stature unzipped the bag so that Oren could see the contents. Oren wasn't surprised to see cash so he counted it inside the bag, nodded and left the room. Oren returned a few minutes later with a similar blue sports bag and placed it next to the one with the cash. The unassuming man looked inside the bag full of morphine, zipped it up, and nodded to Oren. He then left without a word as the transaction was done. Oren zipped up the bag full of cash and took it to the storage to put in the safe that Doug had installed in a cupboard the night his goons broke in. There wasn't anyone in the waiting room, so Oren wasn't worried about being so open with the transaction. The unassuming man was Oren's first; and it went a lot smoother than he expected, yet he still felt quite uneasy. Oren didn't think that Claire was with a patient, but he knocked anyways.

"Hey Claire, you got a minute?"

Claire had her head in her hands. "Sure."

"You alright?" Oren asked.

"I just have a bit of a headache," Claire said.

"So I just did my first exchange if you know what I mean," Oren said.

"It must have gone alright since you're not dead," Claire said.

"It was actually pretty easy. Hardly any talk. Just an exchange. He even had the same blue sports bag that came with the morphine."

Claire rolled her eyes. "Of course. These guys are more organised than the RCMP." Claire was careful how she selected her words, but she still wasn't convinced that they were bugged. She couldn't find anything in her office even after opening up the light switches and ceiling paneling. However, she got all her information from the internet so god only knows how accurate her sleuthing exercise was.

Claire noticed that Oren's hands were shaking. And she believed that he was genuinely scared. Claire took Oren's hand and gave him a worried look.

"It's just adrenaline Claire."

"Do you want some Valium?" Claire asked.

"Not really."

"I have a bit of coke left from the weekend. Would that help?"

Oren's instant reaction was to decline, but then he wasn't sure if he could get through the rest of the day without a little bit of help.

Oren shrugged his shoulders. "Sure, why not? Just a bit though."

Claire opened her purse and took out a sunglasses case. *Interesting hiding spot.* Oren thought. He also noted that when she goes out partying she always takes her clutch. Not that big thing. *Leftover from the weekend, my ass.* He thought to himself. Oren didn't believe Claire, but he didn't care as he had too many other things on his mind. And anyways, she seemed to have her shit together unlike him.

"Thanks." Oren took the coke and made himself a line on Claire's mirror, which was also in her purse. Claire rolled up a $20 and passed it to Oren and he snorted the line. He sat back for a few moments in the chair waiting for the coke to hit him. He was brought back into reality when he heard the door open and close.

"Patient or client?" Claire said.

"If it's one of Doug's goons, do you want me to deal with him?" Oren asked.

"Or her. Don't assume that all of his goons are men." Claire shrugged her shoulders. "Whatever, I'll have to do it sooner or later."

Oren got up and went into the waiting room. A teenager with dark hair was sitting cross-legged in one of the chairs right beside the door. Although she looked a bit rough around the edges, she was quite beautiful with striking brown eyes. He thought he could see First Nations in her. "How can I help you?" Oren asked.

The girl looked up. "Is the woman doctor working here today? I think her name is Dr. Lalonde."

"Sure." Oren assumed that Claire consulted one of her friends about some ailment that could be magically cured by homeopathic treatment. There's no way they'd ever sell prescriptions for narcotics to a minor. Since Claire's door was opened she heard the girl's request. Claire called the girl into her office and shut the door.

"Please have a seat," Claire said as she walked to her desk. Claire noticed holes in the girl's black nylons, which she found to be quite punk rock; but they went very well with her dark, shoulder-length hair and high bangs. She was also wearing a little jean skirt. *Cute.* Claire thought. She was hoping that the girl was only here for homeopathic treatment, but she had a sneaking suspicion that she was about to ask for a prescription; and there is no way that Claire was going to give it to her. This wouldn't be the first time a minor asked Claire for a prescription, and as they all agreed they must act surprised and reaffirm that they only work in a homeopathy clinic.

"I see you already have my name, can I have yours?"

"Molly."

Claire was certain that she was looking for a prescription. "Have you been here before?"

Molly started fidgeting. "No."

"Did your friends tell you about me?"

"No."

"Well, then how do you know my name?"

"I know all your names."

Claire was confused. "What do you mean?"

"I don't really trust men," Molly said.

"No no, that's not what I mean. How do you know us?"

"Doug sent me."

Claire felt sick. It wasn't the morphine thing that caused her stomach to stir. It was because a young lady who was maybe 16 just dropped Doug's name. *What a fucking monster.* Claire thought and her filter was gone.

"How old are you?"

Molly's shyness dissipated. "None of your fucking business, but I'm older than you think."

Claire was irate. "What do you want?"

"I'm here to save your ass. Well, on behalf of Doug." Molly picked up her bag and pulled out a couple of sheets of paper.

"Make sure that you all memorise these faces." Molly placed the two photos, one of a man and one of a woman, in front of Claire. "They're cops and they've been scoping out your clinic for a few weeks."

"How does Doug know this?" Claire asked.

"Look. I can't say much, but one thing that you have to understand is that Doug knows everything. He has eyes everywhere including in the cop shop." Molly stood up. "I gotta go. But those two cops are onto you guys."

After Molly left the clinic Claire picked up the photos of the undercover police officers and walked into Oren's office without even knocking. Right away Oren knew that something was wrong.

"That little girl is one of Doug's and he sent her here to warn us about them." Claire dropped the photos on Oren's desk.

Oren was shocked. "She works for Doug?"

"And apparently she's older than she looks," Claire said.

"Fucking bullshit," Oren said.

"Well, we have bigger shit on our plate right now to deal with," Claire said.

Oren studied the photos. "Are all undercover cops so plain looking?"

Claire rolled her eyes. She couldn't believe that Oren was trying to make a joke. "Do you think they'll pose as buyers?"

"Probably," Oren said.

"For the morphine or prescriptions?" Claire asked.

"I don't know. Either I guess," Oren replied.

"Perfect. A mystery shopper," Claire said.

"Look. If we aren't sure, just stick with the homeopathic front. I'll make copies so that we can keep them in the desks.

"I have no more Valium left and you took the last of my coke," Claire said.

"If we don't learn to deal with this on our own we'll become drug addicts," Oren said.

"And all will fall to shit," Claire said.

"Elegantly put as usual Claire."

"I really wish I could talk to Megs about this," Claire said.

Oren sat up straight in his chair, leaned forward and pointed to Claire. "Don't you dare mention anything to Megs."

"Of course I wouldn't. We'd both be screwed. Sometimes you can be such a knob Oren."

"Sorry for jumping down your throat, but I keep getting a feeling that Megs is suspicious of me. It's as if she knows that something's up," Oren said.

"I'm meeting her for coffee tomorrow morning before my shift here. She'll tell me if she thinks you're hiding something," Claire said.

Oren rolled his eyes. "Of course. There's nothing sacred with you girls. You probably even discuss our sex life."

Someone came into the clinic so Claire got up. "I'll take this one." She then leaned over his desk and whispered. "More cunnilingus...."

Oren just shook his head and tried not to smile. Claire's crudeness, which would shock an old lady, actually made many people laugh. And after what they had been through that day, a bit of comic relief was needed.

Chapter 12

The following day Megs and Claire were having coffee at Cafe Deux Soleil, which was their usual spot. Claire was already on her second Americano, and so far they only talked about the wedding. Claire would try to change the subject in order to ascertain if Megs was actually suspicious of Oren, but within minutes the conversation somehow went back to the wedding.

"I don't know if I should get married in white. Oren seems a bit traditional, but it's my day too. I was thinking more of a baby blue." Claire just kept nodding in agreement as she was trying her best to be a supportive friend, but she just had no interest in wedding stuff, especially when so much had happened in the last few days. Claire's mind kept wandering back to Molly. She desperately wanted to talk to Megs about it, but she knew she could not. She was even afraid to approach the subject matter using a different scenario as she was so worried about slipping up or saying something that would raise suspicion.

"Are you listening to me Claire? I asked you a question."

"Sorry Megs. I'm here. I just didn't sleep very well last night."

"So as I was saying, I've always wanted a destination wedding, but then some of my family members won't be able to afford to go down South or even Hawaii for that matter. What do you think I should do?"

"There are so many gorgeous places in BC, so I just don't see why you wouldn't want to stay here," Claire said.

"You're so right Claire. We could get married in Tofino. I love the island. And anyways, we're going to Colombia soon, so we'll feed our travelling bug that way."

Claire was surprised. "You're both going to Colombia? No one has ever mentioned that to me."

"We only decided at our engagement party. You know that I go every year."

"Yeah. Just not with Oren."

"I don't understand. What's wrong Claire?"

In actual fact Claire was worried about the clinic. Megs often left for a month and she was concerned about running the clinic without Oren for that long.

"Oh no, nothing. I'm happy for you guys. You'll have a great time. I'm just shocked that Oren would go to Colombia in the middle of the summer."

"Yeah. He complained a bit initially but then he came to his senses. It'll only be for three weeks this time."

"How did you talk him into it?" Claire asked.

"I just explained how important this is to me. I want him to see what I do before we get married," Megs said.

"Fair enough." Claire looked at her cell. "I better get to the clinic. If you need any more help with wedding stuff just let me know."

Megs laughed. "You better Claire Bear! Don't forget you're one of my bridesmaids."

Claire started to walk towards the Sky Train station, but as soon as she was out of sight from the cafe she crossed the road and headed towards the pseudo-clinic.

About a few blocks away from the clinic she noticed a parked black SUV with tinted windows. *So fucking obvious.* Claire thought to herself. Pretending not to notice she walked right by the SUV and continued down the road. Initially she thought it was the cops, but then she started to suspect Doug and his goons. Claire snickered at the word goons, which was coined by Oren. *Fits perfectly.* She thought.

As Claire walked into the clinic she noticed one of her regular customers was sitting in the waiting room reading Reader's Digest. "You're early Mrs. Collins."

"Oh hello Dr. Lalonde, I'm having a difficult time sleeping again. Valerian didn't work very well."

"We'll talk about it in a few minutes in my office. I just need to get settled."

"Okay." And Mrs. Collins continued reading the magazine.

Claire was relieved that the only person in the waiting room was a legit homeopathic patient, but she wasn't sure who was with Terry and Oren. There were only two treatment rooms in the clinic, so Claire and Terry shared since they were only at the clinic part-time. Claire knocked on the door. "Hey Terry, are you with a patient?"

"Nope."

Claire rushed into the room and closed the door.

"There's a suspicious vehicle parked about two blocks away."

"Cops?" Terry asked.

Megs shrugged. "I'm not sure if it's the cops or Doug. It's a blacked out SUV."

"Fits both the criminals and the cops nowadays."

"Well, we should assume the worst-case scenario," Claire said.

Terry nodded in agreement. "Cops."

"Is Oren with someone right now?" Claire asked.

"Yeah. It's one of his regulars," Terry replied.

"So in other words, he's not going to walk out of here with a big bag full of morphine while we are being watched by the cops," Claire said.

Terry nodded. "Look. I gotta go. I want to eat some lunch before my shift at my real clinic." Terry started to gather his things, but just before he walked out he turned to Claire and said, "I'll text you what I think after I'm out of sight of the SUV."

"Okay," Claire said.

Oren heard the special knock that they developed if any of them suspected a potential patient as being an undercover cop. Oren answered the door straight away.

Oren could see a concerned look in Terry's eyes. "I'm off for the day. I parked a few blocks west, so hopefully I don't have a ticket. Should have moved my car hours ago," Terry said.

Oren picked up on what Terry was trying to say right away. They were being watched. "You should be fine." And Oren closed the door.

Oren's client didn't seem to notice the randomness of the conversation as he was reading some of his text messages, which kept coming in throughout the entire session. He didn't even bother to put his phone on silent, which annoyed Oren.

"So where were we?" Oren asked.

"I want some more pain medication. I need something stronger than before because it did fuck all for my back."

Oren couldn't stand the guy, but put up with him because he was a regular and brought in a lot of cash. His name was Harley Knowle and was an arrogant, chauvinistic pig. He only had to work for a few months of the year as he was a trucker who'd do a handful of runs across the ice roads up in the Northwest Territories. For the remainder of the year he would spend all his hard-earned cash on pain medication. Harley was genuinely in pain and Oren believed that his back was done in from all those years sitting in a transport. And after his doctor stopped supplying him endlessly with pain medication he turned to crooked doctors like Oren.

"So you need something stronger?"

"Yeah. Way stronger."

"How about morphine?" Oren lowered his voice and leaned towards Harley. "I have a bit left in my supply that I could sell you."

Oren grabbed a piece of paper and wrote the amount down that he thought would be adequate for Harley and how much it would be. Oren slid the paper over to Harley who nodded in approval. "I don't have that cash now, but I can get it to ya."

"I can't give it to you right now anyways," Oren said.

"Why the fuck not?"

"You look like a man who hates cops," Oren said.

"I hate pigs."

"Good." Oren looked down and started to fill in one of the homeopathic sheets and pushed it over to Harley to sign it.

"What's this?" Harley asked.

"This is your chance to do one over on those undercover cops that have been watching us for the past few weeks. We need to get rid of them."

"You're being watched? Shit man, if I would have known I wouldn't have come."

"You haven't done anything wrong and they can't arrest you. And they have nothing on us but some rumours."

Oren wrote out a doctor's note for acupuncture and gave it to Harley.

"Oh and take this too. It's an information sheet on Capsaicin Cream, which is supposed to help your back."

"Fuck this shit man I'm outta here." Harley got up to leave.

"Good luck finding another doctor that will sell you morphine."

Harley quickly sat back down.

"So what do you want me to do doc?"

*****

Harley walked out of the clinic and looked around. He noticed the black SUV straight away. He took his phone out of his back pocket and called his mother. As he waited for her to pick up the phone he kept looking over his shoulder. She was out so he left a message on her voice mail. Harley put his hands in his pockets and started walking west towards the SUV. As he passed the blacked out windows, he tried to peer in from the corner of his eyes. Harley could feel someone watching him. *Fucking pigs.* He thought to himself. After passing the SUV he took out his cell from his back pocket and called his sister. It didn't even ring once before he heard the SUV doors open. Harley hung up his cell, but left it at his ear and continued to walk. He could hear them walking towards him but Harley kept his pace constant.

"Hey! Stop! Police! We have a few questions that we want to ask you." Harley stopped in his tracks and turned around.

"Well if it isn't Mulder and Scully." Harley couldn't resist. Although the female police officer didn't have red hair, it was shoulder length and they were both wearing suits.

Neither of the officers found Harley's quip amusing and they ignored it. "We want to ask you a couple of questions," the male officer said.

"And how about I start? What the hell is this about?" Harley said.

This time it was the female officer's turn to speak. "There have been some reports that suspicious activity may be going on in that clinic and you just walked out of there."

"That homeopathic clinic? Are you insane?" Harley said.

The female officer shook her head in disbelief. "You expect us to believe that you're into holistic medicine?"

"Why not? Because I'm a middle-aged bearded trucker?" Harley was genuinely upset with this stereotype. "I've suffered from chronic back pain for years and I'm sick and tired of taking codeine and other mind-numbing shit. So as I've been advised by my mother, I'm getting acupuncture done."

"They do acupuncture in there?" the female officer asked.

Harley opened up his jacket pocket and pulled out the doctor's note. "No. I needed a proper MD to write me up a doctor's note, so that I can get this covered by my extended health-care plan."

"And what does that paper say?" the female officer asked.

Harley was holding the information page in his other hand. He gave it to the officer. "Capsaicin Cream," the female officer said. She shrugged her shoulders and handed back the doctor's note and information page to Harley.

"Sorry about that sir and thank you for your time. I hope you have a good day."

Harley wanted to say a few more things to the two police officers, but he bit his tongue. "Yeah. You too," he said sarcastically and continued walking towards his pickup that was parked on the same block as the SUV.

The police officers were already in the clinic by the time Harley started his car. He hoped that Oren had his story straight because unlike the 1980s, it was so hard to find crooked doctors.

*****

Oren was nervously sitting at his desk with the office door ajar waiting for the police to come in. He already gave the warning knock on Claire's door but since she was with a legit patient, she didn't seem too worried. His phone buzzed as he received a text message. As Oren suspected it was from Harley "they bought it." Oren quickly responded "meet at 7 as discussed." As soon as his text went through, he deleted all of his messages on his cell. He didn't want to risk anything. He heard the door open and two suits walked in, one male and one female. They were the same faces that were on Molly's photocopied headshots. Oren got up from his desk and walked into the waiting room. "How can I help you?"

The male police officer spoke first. "This is Detective Simpson and I'm Detective Mazis."

Oren tried his best to look confused.

"We want to ask you and your colleagues a couple of questions," Detective Mazis said.

"Well, Dr. Lalonde is with a patient at the moment, but I would be more than happy to answer your questions."

"We will also have to speak with Dr. Lalonde when she is finished with her patient," Detective Mazis said.

Oren nodded. "Please have a seat in my office."

It was Detective Simpson's turn to speak. "So I hear that this is a homeopathic clinic."

Oren nodded.

"How many patients do you see per day?"

"I don't know. It varies." Oren crossed his legs and started to open up some of his drawers. "I could look through the files and give you an accurate figure if you like."

"We're just looking for an estimate," Detective Simpson said.

"Some days we may only see 10 patients and other days we could be as busy as 30 or 40 patients," Oren said.

"We've been watching your place for a couple of weeks and there seems to be a lot of activity here."

"Well, Mondays and Tuesday are always quiet in comparison...." Oren stopped short and raised his voice. "You've been watching us?"

The detectives didn't say anything, which made Oren even angrier.

"Why were you watching my clinic? I deserve to know what this is all about!"

Detective Mazis took a photo out of his jacket pocket.

"Have you ever seen this person before?"

Oren looked at the photo. It was a very alive picture of the dopey-looking punk that Doug had killed.

"You know who this is?" Detective Simpson asked.

Oren knew that he couldn't lie as his face lit up with recognition when he looked at the photo. "Well, I don't even know his name, but he's come in here a few times. What's this about?"

"His body was found nearly a month ago. He was murdered."

Oren became quite nervous as he wondered if they found the illegal prescriptions that he prescribed for the little weasel.

"That's awful but what does that have to do with us?" Oren asked.

"During our investigation we were interviewing his circle of friends, and they mentioned that he would often come to this clinic to get drugs."

Oren was relieved and decided it was time to get into character. He started shaking his head. "That druggie scumbag used to come into this clinic trying to persuade us to write him prescriptions for narcotics. I tried to talk him into going to re-hab not sell him drugs!" Oren looked straight at the detectives. "We are a well-respected holistic clinic, not some back alley drug dispenser."

Detective Mazis put the photo back in his jacket pocket. "We are not insinuating anything. We are just trying to follow a potential lead. Now can you tell us anything about Jonathan Hart aka Heartless Jon?"

Oren tried not to laugh. "Heartless Jon?"

"That's his street name. Most drug dealers have street names."

"Oh," Oren said.

"Can you tell us anything?" Detective Mazis asked once again.

"Look. I'm really sorry. All I can say is that I dealt with him a few times, tried to help him and then when I realised that he was a lost soul I gave up."

"How about the other doctors? Did they have any run-ins with Heartless?"

"I don't know, but you can talk to Dr. Lalonde once she's done with her patient," Oren said.

Detective Mazis opened up his wallet and gave his business card to Oren. "If you think of anything else, please give us a call."

"Of course," Oren said.

The detectives got up and took their seat in the waiting room. Initially Oren was annoyed that Claire was taking her sweet time with her patient, but then he realised that perhaps she was doing it on purpose. In other words, she was putting her legit patient on display for the detectives to see. A few minutes later the door opened and Mrs. Collins walked out of the treatment room.

Oren was quite surprised that the detectives didn't stop to question Mrs. Collins, but rather they just watched her leave the clinic. As soon as the door closed behind Mrs. Collins the detectives got up and walked towards Claire's office. Although Oren knew that Claire could sense the detectives at the door, he was amazed that she just kept her head down while writing notes.

"Just two seconds. I need to write everything down before I forget," Claire said.

Finally, after what felt like an eternity, Claire looked up. "Thank you for your patience. How can I help you?"

Oren quickly jumped in. "This is Detective Simpson and Detective Mazis, and they would like to ask you a few questions."

Detective Mazis looked straight at Oren. "We can take it from here."

Oren nodded and went back into his office.

"Please take a seat," Claire said.

The two detectives closed the door and sat down looking straight at Claire.

"We're detectives at the Vancouver Police Department. We're currently investigating a homicide and we have a few questions," Detective Simpson said.

"Homicide?" Claire asked.

Detective Simpson nodded.

The first thought that jumped into Claire's mind was that they found their prescriptions on the kid's murdered body. Claire decided to play dumb.

"What do you mean homicide? Like synonymous to murder?

"Dr. Lalonde, please calm down. We just need to ask you a couple of very simple questions," Detective Simpson said.

Claire nodded.

Detective Mazis took the photo out of his jacket pocket. "Can you identify this person?"

Claire wished she had a few minutes with Oren to get their stories straight. Both of them assumed that the only reason the police would see them is for the suspicion of dealing narcotics or for writing illegal prescriptions, not for murder.

Claire guessed that Oren was honest about knowing this person.

"He looks familiar but he wasn't one of my patients," Claire said.

"So he was a patient at this clinic?" Detective Simpson asked.

Claire was worried that she just said the wrong thing.

"I assumed he was because I've seen him in the waiting room before."

"What was he doing?"Detective Simpson asked. Claire looked sheepishly at her. "Waiting I guess. I'm sorry, but he wasn't one of my patients."

Detective Simpson looked straight into Claire's eyes. "So you're telling me that Dr. O'Brian never mentioned Jonathan Hart to you?"

A light went on in Claire's head and she read between the lines.

"No. Dr. O'Brian never mentioned this Jonathan to me, he only warned me."

"Warned you about what?" Detective Simpson asked.

"Not to talk to him. Not to give him what he wanted." Claire sat back in her chair and waited for the detectives to ask more questions.

The detectives looked at each other and got up. "Thank you for your time Dr. Lalonde."

Claire wasn't sure if her story matched what Oren said or if they conflicted. She followed them out of her office, and Oren joined them straight away in the waiting room.

The detectives shook their hands. "Thank you for your time but I would like to reiterate that if you think of anything else, please contact us straight away," Detective Mazis said.

As soon as the detectives closed the door Claire followed Oren into his office.

"I hope we were on the same wavelength. I assumed you told the detectives that you knew that kid," Claire said.

"He was known as Heartless Jon," Oren said.

Claire rolled her eyes as she thought those street names were always so cheesy. "Can we close up shop early today?"

Oren nodded. "I'm doing a drop off anyways."

"Me too," Claire said.

"Jesus, you've sold a lot," Oren said.

"I have a lot of desperate friends," Claire said.

"It's nearly over. There's not much morphine left," Oren said.

Claire grinned. "This is only the beginning my dear friend."

Oren closed his eyes. "I damn well hope not."

*****

"Here's your Quarter Pounder with fries."

Oren grabbed the food from the window and placed it on the passenger seat.

"Could I get an extra paper bag?" "Oren asked.

"Certainly sir."

Oren took the paper bag and also placed it on the passenger seat. He drove away and parked in a stall at the far end of the parking lot. He opened the empty McDonald's bag and placed it on the floor of the passenger's side. He grabbed the morphine from under the passenger's seat and put it in the empty McDonald's bag. Oren looked around and he saw Harley sitting at a table outside, slowly eating a hamburger. Oren grabbed the bag, got out of the car and walked towards Harley. Oren sat down in front of Harley and stole one of his fries. He placed the McDonald's paper bag full of morphine on the table and grabbed the identical bag beside it, which was full of money. Oren looked around and it was apparent that no one was even watching them. He grabbed Harley's money, got up, and walked back to his car. After taking a couple of breaths, Oren turned the ignition and drove away.

As Oren sat at a red light a homeless man approached his window to beg for money. Oren opened his window and gave his Quarter Pounder meal to the homeless man. The light turned green. "I don't want this fucking shit, I want some money." Oren bit his tongue and rolled up his window, squealing his tires as he drove off.

Chapter 13

It has been less than 24 hours since Oren met with the detectives and he couldn't shake the image of Jon "Heartless" Hart out of his head. He decided to go for a long run to try and clear his mind. Since the dopey-looking kid was named, Oren was having a hard time coping with his death; and he didn't understand why. Last night he couldn't sleep as he somehow felt partly responsible. Questions would run through his mind such as *if I had never opened the clinic would the kid still be alive?* And *should I have been more careful in the selection of my clientele?* However, the big question that brought out much fear in Oren was: How many others are dealing our drugs? Oren started to realise that it was only a matter of time before they would get caught.

Oren started to get a cramp in his leg, so he slowed down to a walking pace and headed for a bench. As Oren stretched his leg he looked out onto the harbour and North Vancouver. Oren's favourite running route was along the sea wall, and a couple of times per month he would run around Stanley Park. He used to do this route more often, but since he opened up the pseudo-clinic, he didn't have as much time for many extracurricular activities.

Oren started running again. Earlier that day the remainder of the morphine was bought by someone who organised the pick up through Doug or one of his affiliates. He brought in the perfect amount of cash to buy the remainder of the shipment. This didn't surprise Oren, since he knew very well that Doug's goons would do an inventory when they would pick up the cash in the safe in the middle of the night. However, Oren was never sure when that was as they would come and clear the safe any random night of the week. There seemed to be no schedule. But then Oren wondered if randomness was indeed purposeful. Oren was tired of thinking about the whole Doug thing and wanted to focus on his running. He took his iPod out of his pocket and selected Mumford and Sons as that band really pumped him up. Oren chuckled to himself as he thought of his recent conversation with Megs just before he left their house to go for a run. She poked fun because she thought he had the world's most boring music collection on his iPod, and couldn't understand how it could energize him. She offered her iPod, but he pretended to be offended. In reality he didn't give a shit. Megs was heavily into instrumental music, electronic, trance, drum and base, anything that didn't have any singing it in which Oren hated. She would rant and rave about Bonobo, Explosions in the Sky and that band with an exclamation mark in their name, and he just didn't get it. They had a lot in common but music wasn't it. Often they would sit at home in silence as they couldn't find a happy music medium.

As Oren passed the bronze statue of "Girl in a Wetsuit" he decided to push a little harder and he increased his pace. Oren noticed that someone was close behind him, so he quickened his pace even more. The person behind him did the same. Oren pushed a bit harder and once again the person behind him followed suit. Initially, Oren was frightened as he was certain that he was being followed. But then again, there were people around who were also using the path. Oren was tired of this game so he started to slow down to the point he was running next to the person. He turned his head and his heart jumped. It was Doug.

"Thank god you're slowing down. I'm so fed up of trying to catch up to you," Doug said.

"Why are you following me?" Oren asked.

"Can we slow it down a bit?" Doug asked.

Oren slowed down to a light jog. "This is good. I want to keep running but I don't want a heart attack," Doug said.

"So why are you following me?" Oren asked again.

"I wouldn't say I'm following you. I need to talk to you and this is the safest way."

Oren ripped his headphones out of his ears and shoved his iPod into his pocket.

"So what is it then?" Oren asked.

"Don't you want to get paid Oren?" Doug asked.

"I assumed you'd put the cash in the safe tonight," Oren said.

"Well, you assumed correctly. Not sure about tonight, though. It will be there sometime in the next few days; we just have to ensure that none of the pigs are watching your place." Doug started to chuckle.

"What's so funny?" Oren asked.

"I heard that a couple of detectives paid you a visit yesterday."

"That was because of you," Oren said.

"But this is good news. They weren't watching you because of your carelessness," Doug said.

Oren was getting frustrated with Doug, so he stopped jogging and started to walk in the opposite direction.

"Keep up with me Oren. Our discussion is not yet over."

Oren had a flashback of Heartless' picture and his slit throat, so he quickly caught up with Doug.

"What do you mean I was being careless?" Oren asked.

"You've been writing prescriptions out to any fool that would walk into your clinic." Doug wiped some sweat off of his brow. "Heartless wasn't the only one, and you are so lucky that the cops haven't found your prescription bottles yet."

Oren was shocked that Doug just described what he was thinking of earlier, but then he realised that his mistakes have been pretty damn obvious. It was in Doug's best interest to have a chat with Oren about this subject matter.

Oren started focussing hard on Lion's Gate Bridge, which was getting bigger and bigger as they ran towards its base.

"Since you are working for me, I want you to stop your illegal prescription operation as it's too risky. All it will take is one client to tell the wrong person and your detective friends will be back. Although this time it may be the RCMP."

Another jab that pissed Oren off, but instead he swallowed his pride as he knew that Doug was very dangerous. Oren shook his head. "We don't want to do this anymore."

"Not even an immense amount of money will tempt you?" Doug asked.

"We have enough. Please Doug. We don't want to be part of this anymore."

Doug's face darkened. "I will tell you when you are done."

"We don't want to do this forever Doug. We're not real criminals," Oren said.

"I'll ignore your ridiculous criminal comment, but I never do business with the same people for too long."

"What do you mean?" Oren asked.

"I need you for two more jobs. After you successfully complete the third and final job our contract will cease to exist, and you can live a long and happy life with all your riches," Doug said.

Oren looked up at the Lion's Gate Bridge as they passed underneath it.

"Tonight I have another shipment coming in, and we'll have a similar set up as before but with different pricing."

"What's the pricing?" Oren asked.

"Those details will be in an envelope that we'll leave in the safe after we drop off the shipment."

The men continued running in silence. Once they reached the first set of stairs that led to the tea house, Doug peeled off without even saying good-bye.

Oren started to sprint. He wanted to get his run over and done with, but he knew he had quite a few kilometers left. His heart started to beat and his insides began to burn. He could see Second Beach coming up in the distance and he pushed harder. The lactic acid started to build up in his legs, but he ignored it and ran even faster. Oren veered off the path onto the sand and collapsed on his hands and knees. He started to throw up but only bile was coming out. Once he was done throwing up he lied on his back and closed his eyes. Oren felt that he no longer was in control of his life, but then he kept reminding himself that he would only have to do this twice more and Doug will leave him alone. God, he hoped that Doug was a man of his word.

*****

It was nearly 6 o'clock and Claire was tired of being in the clinic. Oren left a few hours previous so that he could rush home and grab his running gear. *What kind of freak runs around Stanley Park for fun?* Claire thought. As she locked up the clinic she heard a car door slam. Her heart started to beat fast and she spun around. She looked up and down the street and saw a woman help her kids out of a white mini-van. "Fucking soccer mom," Claire mumbled to herself and walked towards the Sky Train. As she passed a lane she noticed a black SUV parked up it. Still full of adrenalin she started to walk towards it, assuming it was the cops again. Claire looked into the passenger window and the car was empty. There was a cross dangling from the rear-view mirror. "Doug?" Claire asked herself. She started to feel nervous and walked behind the SUV and noticed the Ichthys symbol on the bumper. Claire was relieved. "It's just a bible thumper."

As Claire started walking back to the main road she began to feel nervous again. *What if this is how the cartel disguises their vehicles?* Claire started to pick up her pace as she walked towards the Sky Train. Once reaching the chaos of

Commercial Drive, Claire thought she would feel safer, but that was far from the truth. Her heart was racing and she wanted to get the hell out of there. There was a gap in the traffic, so Claire took advantage of that and ran to the other side of the road and into the station. As she was running up the stairs she could hear her train so she pushed her legs to go faster. She didn't even wait for the people to fully vacate the train before pushing her way in and collapsing in a seat. When the Sky Train departed, Claire took a deep breath and tried to relax. She turned and looked out the window towards the mountains. Claire closed her eyes as her heartbeat went back to normal. When she finally opened her eyes, she focussed in on the reflections of the passengers in her window; and that's when she saw him. A scary-looking man was standing near the doors boring holes into the back of Claire's head. It took a lot for Claire to be courageous, but she kept calm and studied the man's reflection. He seemed huge and was wearing a leather jacket and leather gloves. She felt queasy. The train started slowing down at the Main Street Station and the doors opened. The door chimes started to ring and Claire jumped up from her seat and ran out of the train as the doors closed behind her. Claire casually walked down the stairs, and she thought she could feel the man continue to stare at her. Although, in reality, she had no clue if this was indeed the case since she was too afraid to look back at the train.

Claire walked north on Main Street and as the sound of police sirens passed her she started to feel much safer. If anything happened to her here there would be so many witnesses. Claire was about a 15-minute walk from her place, but she was afraid to go home as she was worried that the man would be waiting for her. She took her cell out of her purse and tried to phone Oren, but it went directly onto his voice mail. Claire didn't know where to go and she absolutely refused to see Megs. She'd see that Claire was upset and would start asking loads of questions giving her the third degree. With friends, Claire was a terrible liar and Megs could see through her lies anyways. She just couldn't risk accidentally saying anything that would raise suspicion. Not when she was about to break down. "What to do?" Claire asked herself.

Claire started to hear music, which was coming from the London Pub. And Claire went in and directly walked towards the washroom, which was located at the back of the pub. Claire stared at her face in the washroom mirror for a few moments. She was flushed and the dark rings around her eyes were quite pronounced. She was unable to sleep much in the last few weeks, but she kept forgetting to steal some sleeping pills from the clinic. Claire opened up her purse and pulled out her sunglasses case, which was used to hide her narcotics. She desperately needed some Valium, so she popped a couple of pills in her mouth and drank from the tap. She stared at her reflection for a few moments and started to think that maybe she was being paranoid. She wondered how much detail can actually be seen from merely a window reflection. However, Claire was certain that the man was wearing black gloves. This didn't make any sense since it was the middle of June.

Claire's thoughts were interrupted by another woman walking into the washroom, which was her cue to leave.

As Claire was walking towards the door to leave the pub, she noticed Detective Mazis at the bar drinking a pint of lager. Claire quickly changed her mind about leaving and took the empty seat next to the detective. Claire hung her purse on the back of the chair and smiled at the bartender. "What can I get you?"

"What's your house red?" Claire asked.

"Jackson Triggs. It's their cabernet sauvignon."

"I'll have a glass of that please," Claire said.

"Thought I recognised that voice," Detective Mazis said.

Claire turned and smiled at the detective, who was still focussed on the television behind the bar.

"I rushed in to use the washroom, but as I was leaving I saw you nursing your pint. Thought you needed a bit of company."

"Kinda hard not to notice with the way you flung that door open."

Claire shrugged her shoulders. "I really had to pee."

Detective Mazis took another sip of his beer still looking at the television.

A few awkward minutes went by without the detective even looking at Claire. Finally she had enough.

"Whatever. Fuck you and your bullshit cop attitude. I sat down here thinking you needed some company. You clearly don't, so I'll take my drink elsewhere."

Claire grabbed her stuff and walked over to an empty table. She sat down and took out her smartphone and went on her Facebook account. She needed something to occupy her mind as she waited for both the Valium and red wine to kick in. And reading her News Feed, which had loads of updates of her friend's mundane lives, seemed the perfect way to help her forget about the scare she had on the Sky Train.

As Claire was analysing the photos of an old high school friend who was heavily pregnant she felt someone hovering over top of her and assumed it was a server. Claire looked up and was shocked to see Detective Mazis.

"May I sit down?"

"Sure, as long as you left your attitude at the bar."

Detective Mazis smiled. "Sorry about that. I've had a really hard few days. Actually, make that a few months."

Claire wasn't impressed, especially since he and his partner grilled her a few days prior. "Me too."

"Look. I'm sorry. That wasn't fair. I was being a dick," Detective Mazis said.

It wasn't often that Claire would hear a cop admit his shortcomings, so she was quite satisfied with his apology.

Claire smiled and the detective took a seat.

"Wow. Someone is about to pop," Detective Mazis said as he looked at the photo that Claire still had up on her smartphone, which was lying face up on the table.

"I know. Fucking scary, isn't it? She's huge!"

All of a sudden Claire felt a bit embarrassed. She wasn't sure if Detective Mazis was taken aback by her potty mouth or her astonishment of the size of her pregnant friend.

The detective started laughing. "You don't have any kids do you?"

Claire shook her head.

"You look confused. Did I offend you?"

"Oh no. You didn't." Claire took a sip of her wine. "Actually, I thought you'd criticize me for making such a statement and being a doctor."

"Actually, that's a good point," Detective Mazis said.

"This girl not only was the valedictorian for our year, but she was also crowned prom queen."

"And?" Detective Mazis asked.

"Fuck, I sound so catty. She used to be so obsessed with her body and image. So when I see her proudly posting pictures of her giant, naked belly on Facebook I'm a bit shocked."

"You certainly have a mouth of a sailor," Detective Mazis said.

"Okay detective. If you are going to sit here and criticize me, then I would rather be alone with my phone criticizing my friends on Facebook."

"Firstly, I'm off duty, so please call me Evan. And secondly, I think your sailor's mouth is kinda cute."

Claire wondered if that was his attempt at a pick up line. And screwing a cop was on her bucket list so she decided to go with it. "Cute? Now that's a first."

Evan started to look more relaxed. "So tell me. Is there something going on between you and Dr. O'Brian?"

Now Claire was certain that Evan was interested in her. "God no! He's engaged."

"Sorry. I was a bit forward."

"It's okay. We're both adults here." Claire took another sip of her wine and smiled at Evan again. She studied his square jaw line and followed it up to his cute little ears. His hair was a nice chestnut colour with the perfect amount of grey, which made him more distinguished looking. His eyes were dark brown with ridiculously long eyelashes. And when he smiled it would light up a room. So dreamy Claire thought to herself, *but this was the same dick that grilled her the day before with his bitch partner.*

"So tell me Evan. Why did you guys pick on our clinic?"

"We didn't pick on your clinic. We were following a lead."

"Some low-life drug dealer who is probably messed up on drugs himself tells you a load of bullshit and you call that a lead?"

Evan shook his head. "Jesus doc, I came in here to get some peace and quiet and forget about this dead end of a case; and now you're grilling me."

"Look. You and your partner scared the shit out of us, insinuating that we were involved with some big drug ring and then the murder thing."

Claire wasn't sure if Evan looked upset or annoyed.

"I'm sorry if we scared you, but rest assured your clinic as well as the others all came up clean."

"Others?"

"Heartless' little circle of friends dropped the names of a series of clinics, yours being one of them."

"You just told me too much, didn't you?"

"Yes."

"Sorry. I shouldn't have let my emotions get the better of me. That was very unprofessional."

Evan shrugged his shoulders. "Can I call you Claire?"

"Yeah. Of course."

"Well, technically, speaking with you off duty like this is also very unprofessional. But since you're no longer a suspect, and compounded by the fact that I was rude to you earlier, I thought what the hell?"

"So deciphering what you just said, you are willing to break some rules to chat with me."

Evan raised his glass. "I'll cheers to that."

*****

A few hours later Claire was in Evan's house unbuckling his belt. "Do you have any handcuffs?"

Evan's eyes lit up. "I love that kinky shit."

Claire reached into Evan's pants and she felt his massive cock. He was as horny and she was. Evan and Claire slowly moved into his bedroom clumsily taking off each other clothes.

Evan stopped for a few moments and looked at Claire's body. "God you're sexy." He then picked her up and put her on his bed. "Hey. Where are you going?" Claire asked.

He went into his closet and came back with some handcuffs. "As requested doctor." He raised Claire's arms above her head and handcuffed her to his metal headboard. Claire was getting more aroused by the second. Evan started kissing her and slowly worked down her body. Once he reached her pussy she started to moan. Claire was about to climax when he stopped and put his cock inside of her. "Oh my god you're huge!" Claire said. Evan started thrusting,

115

slowly at first, gradually increasing his tempo. Claire closed her eyes and turned her head towards the night table. "How does that feel doc?" Evan asked.

When Claire opened her eyes she met face-to-face with a pretty blond lady and two cute little girls. "We're being watched!"

Evan stopped thrusting. "What?" And he followed Claire's line of sight to the picture of his wife and two kids on his nightstand.

"You're married?" Claire asked.

"Well, not exactly," Evan said.

"Get off of me," Claire said.

"C'mon Claire."

"Get the fuck off of me."

Evan got up and removed the handcuffs.

"I can't believe I was so blind. Your wife obviously still lives in this room. Her stuff is everywhere."

"Seriously. I can explain," Evan said.

"Where are they?" Claire asked.

Evan shrugged his shoulders.

Claire started collecting her clothes. "Where's my shirt?"

"Probably in the living room."

"Look. Doing married guys isn't a big deal for me. But when kids are involved. Well, that's just wrong."

Still completely nude Evan followed Claire into the living room. "C'mon Claire. We're separating. That's why they aren't here. They are staying with my mother-in-law."

As Claire was buttoning up her blouse she noticed the light flashing on the answering machine. She couldn't help herself so she pushed the button.

"Hi Daddy! It's Moira! We've seen Cinderella! She's so pretty. Lindy wants to say...." Evan stopped the machine.

"They're at Disneyland?" Claire asked.

Evan looked upset. "No, on a Princess cruise."

"When I found out that my father cheated on my mom, I never spoke to him again. And that was back in 1996. Don't screw this up Evan."

And Claire walked out of his house slamming the door behind her.

Chapter 14

Oren took the last two days off and used the excuse that he was helping Megs with wedding stuff. In reality he just needed a break from the clinic. He wanted to take another day off, but he received a text from Terry. It was somewhat coded, but Oren could tell something was up and guessed that Doug's shipment was delivered.

It was after opening hours, but the clinic was still locked. Oren unlocked the door and followed Claire and Terry's voices to the storage room.

"Hey guys," Oren said.

Both Claire and Terry were startled.

"We didn't even hear you come in," Terry said.

"So what do we have here?" Oren asked.

"Fentanyl," Terry said and he handed a sample to Oren.

"A transdermal patch," Oren said as he analysed the sample.

Claire rolled her eyes and turned to Oren. "Thank you, captain fucking obvious!"

"What's up with you?" Oren asked.

"Have you ever prescribed fentanyl before?" Claire asked.

Oren and Terry both shook their heads.

"Of course you didn't. The only time we ever give our patients these patches is in the hospital when they are on death's door," Claire said.

"Now you're being condescending Claire. I've given this to some of my terminally ill patients who weren't responding to morphine," Oren said.

"And why was that?" Claire asked.

Oren was getting annoyed. "Claire, we're not goddamn idiots here, we all know that fentanyl is stronger than morphine. So what's your point?"

"Fentanyl is one hundred times stronger than morphine. So in other words, we can only sell this shit to a client who has a high tolerance to opiates. If we aren't careful and just sell this to anyone, they'll overdose and die."

"Claire's right. Can we rely solely on the people who Doug sends?" Terry asked.

"I don't think so Terry. Doug gave us a deadline to sell this entire supply," Oren said.

"One month?" Terry asked.

"Yeah," Oren replied.

"I have an idea," Claire said. "We just sell the fentanyl to our clients who we have been prescribing various opiates for and selling the morphine too."

"Oh really? I was thinking that we should sell it to people like Mrs. Collins instead," Oren said.

"Screw you and your sarcasm, Oren. I'm just trying to come up with some ideas here."

Oren started pacing back and forth in the storage room. "Let me get this straight. We have no choice but to sell this to our clients. However, we must be selective to ensure that they are long-term opiate users."

"But how do we know they have a decent build-up of opiates in their bodies?" Terry said and shook his head. "I mean, when I was giving fentanyl to my patients, they were taking morphine and other pain medication for weeks. And to be honest with you, most of them were on death's door anyways, so I was trying to make it as painless as possible."

"Can't we just be honest with our clients?" Claire asked.

"What do you mean?" Oren said.

Claire waved one of the patches in the air. "Tell them how strong and potentially lethal this innocent-looking patch is. And we tell them to cut it in half." Claire analysed the patch. "Maybe even quarters."

"No. The gel will come out and it could increase the dosage and cause them to overdose. The patch in its whole form will allow a slow release. We just have to screen our patients and ask more questions about their opiate usage," Oren said.

Terry looked worried. "So we have to trust them? Trust that they are regular oxycodone or morphine users? I don't want blood on my hands."

"None of us do, but I don't think we have a choice. Trusting our clients is our only viable option," Oren said.

Claire's face lit up. "One of my colleagues works at a clinic near East Hastings. Most of her work consists of handing out methadone to druggies. Perhaps we could each do a couple of shifts a week there to help sell our supply of fentanyl. Then we don't have to worry about selling it to our existing clients."

Oren and Terry were speechless and just stared at Claire.

"What? They are always looking for doctors to work in the clinics geared towards the likes of those in Downtown Eastside. I'd even volunteer."

"I really hope that was a joke Claire. Most of those so-called druggies who are living in Canada's poorest postal code go to those clinics because they want to kick their drug habit," Oren said.

Claire rolled her eyes and looked at Terry for his input.

"Seriously Claire, I wouldn't be able to sleep at night if I did that. It's like going to an AA meeting handing out free vodka shooters instead of coffee and cake. It's just wrong."

"I agree Terry. But how is it any different to illegally prescribing narcotics to our clients? They are desperate, too."

Oren jumped in. "Number one, they come to us. Number two, they are in control. Number three, we know who they are and where they live. Number four...."

Claire interrupted. "Actually, you're up to five."

"Number five then. They aren't trying to kick their habit. Number six, they don't live on the streets because of their habit. Number seven, they don't sell their bodies because of their habit. Number eight..."

"Okay. Shut up Oren. I get your point," Claire said.

All three of the doctors sat in silence for a few minutes.

Finally, Terry broke the silence. "So our safest bet is to trust our existing clients and carefully screen them. Right?"

"I'm afraid so," Oren said.

*****

"Are you shitting me, doc? That much for a stack of nicotine patches?" Harley was not amused with what Oren had to offer.

"I need morphine. My back is in so much pain that I can't even sleep at night. It's driving me crazy."

Oren waited patiently for Harley to finish ranting.

"Fentanyl is one hundred times more powerful than morphine. This transdermal patch will slowly release fentanyl into your body. It's superior to morphine," Oren said.

"I find this hard to believe," Harley said.

"How about this? I'll give you one patch to try tonight. And if it meets your expectations, text me the same message as before," Oren said.

"And do you want to do the exchange at McDonald's again?" Harley asked.

"Sure. But a different McDonald's just to be safe. How about the one near Renfrew Sky Train station?" Oren said.

"Yeah. That's fine. Same time tomorrow if and only if you get my text," Harley said.

"I'll be expecting it." Oren stood up and shook Harley's hand. "I'm that confident in this product."

Harley smiled and walked out of the office. As he opened the clinic door he nearly bumped into a man wearing sunglasses, a baseball hat and carrying a blue bag. The man stepped away from the door and let Harley out.

So fucking obvious. Harley thought to himself.

The man then walked into the clinic and quietly sat in the waiting room.

A few minutes later Oren walked out of his office and saw the man. Keeping his sunglasses on, he followed Oren into his office closing the door behind him.

The transaction was quick and no words were exchanged, which was the way Oren preferred.

Doug seemed to be sending double the amount of people for pickups and the fentanyl was going quick. Oren had no doubt that he would meet the one-month deadline.

Chapter 15

"Oh my god, this is good fucking pizza!" Claire said as she crammed another slice into her mouth.

"You certainly put ass in class Claire!" Oren said, causing Terry to burst out laughing. The banter between Claire and Oren was back in full swing after a hiatus due to the stress with their drug business and their dealings with Doug.

"God I feel good," Oren said. "I haven't felt this good in weeks."

"We need some more shots!" Claire said and she caught the attention of their server.

"Could we get another round of tequila shots?" Claire asked.

The server retuned with three shots of tequila, three slices of lemon and a salt shaker.

They all picked up their shots and Oren was the first to speak. "To us!"

Claire jumped in. "And being fucking rich!"

They all slammed back their tequilas.

Claire stood up to go to the bathroom and quickly sat back down in her chair as she lost her balance.

"You are so cut off," Terry said.

"You're right. I should go home. I have a night shift tomorrow at the hospital," Claire said.

"What the hell are you doing working tomorrow?" Oren asked.

"It's a favour for a colleague." Claire was slurring her words.

Claire grabbed her phone out of her purse. "I can't see straight. Can one of you call me a taxi?"

Terry took out his phone. "I have to jet as well. You're kinda on my way so we can share a cab."

Claire nodded and stumbled to the washroom.

"How are you getting home?" Terry asked.

"I think I'm going to walk. I need some air. Also, Megs is working stupid late tonight preparing for her trip to Colombia."

"Aren't you going, too?"

Oren nodded. "Yep."

"When's your flight?" Terry asked.

"The end of the week, but Megs has quite a bit of organisation to do." Oren shrugged his shoulders and sat back in his seat. "It is technically a work trip and I'm just tagging along."

"C'mon. It'll be an adventure," Terry said.

"I'd rather be sipping margaritas at a swim up bar."

Terry laughed. "Your stereotypical roles are so reversed in that relationship of yours!"

Claire was stumbling towards their table.

"You look after Claire and I'll look after the bill," Oren said.

"You sure?"

"What's a couple hundred bucks now?" Oren said.

"True," Terry said. "I'll get the tab next time."

Terry helped Claire put on her jacket and escorted her out of Falconetti's.

Oren slowly finished his beer and looked at his watch. It was barely midnight, but they started drinking quite early in the evening and had a ridiculous amount of shots. That morning a huge sum of money was left in the safe, which translated to their payment for selling all the fentanyl. Oren wasn't sure how he was going to launder the money, but apparently Terry's unethical lawyer was more than happy to help them out for a reasonable cut. It looked like they may re-invest the money into their clinic or even buy another using the same homeopathic front. Oren was worried that at one point Megs would find out about their holistic clinic and see through it. So far he has been lucky as Megs' mind has been occupied planning the trip to Colombia and more importantly their wedding. *But what would happen once all the dust settles?* Oren thought to himself.

"Here's the bill," the server said.

Oren paid by cash, got up and left the restaurant.

As Oren started walking home he heard the buzz of the Sky Train go by. It was a relatively warm night, but Oren was no longer looking forward to the 40-minute walk home, so instead he headed towards the Sky Train station on Commercial Drive and Broadway.

As Oren made his way up the stairs he was startled by the sound of a vehicle squealing its tires. He looked over his shoulder and noticed a black SUV drive away.

Oren's first thought was Doug, but then the undercover cops used the same vehicle. Oren decided that he was just being paranoid and continued to the platform to wait for the train.

Oren loved the efficiency of the Sky Train. Within 15 minutes he was nearly home. As his apartment came into view he noticed the black SUV parked in front. His heart started to pound; but he wasn't going to let anyone shake him, especially not Doug. As Oren walked past the SUV he noticed the driver's window was opened. The driver exhaled his cigarette and looked directly at Oren. "Get in."

"No," Oren said.

"Get the fuck in!"

Oren stood his ground and didn't move.

"You're wasting my time doctor."

Oren didn't move.

The back door of the SUV opened.

"Our boss wants to talk to you. Now get in."

At that point Oren knew that there were more people in the car. He was outnumbered and had no choice but to abide.

Oren got into the car and as soon as he closed the door the driver took off.

The man next to him held up a bandana. "We have to blindfold you."

Once again Oren knew he had no choice so he let the man blindfold him.

After many turns, Oren felt that they were on the Trans-Canada Highway heading out of the city. Oren guessed eastwards because the road was fairly straight and they were driving for some time. Oren started to count in his head so that he could keep track of how far they were driving. He assumed they were travelling at around 120 km/h. After about a 20 minutes Oren guessed they were in Coquitlam, but the car did not slow.

Oren estimated that they were driving for around an hour or so when the SUV finally started to slow down and exit off the highway. He guessed they were near Abbotsford.

After a few more turns they reached a gravel road.

Oren started to get nervous. "Where the hell are we going?"

But no one answered.

The SUV finally came to a stop and everyone got out of the car. Oren waited for someone to open his door and escort him out.

Still blindfolded, Oren was led into a building and was ordered to stay still.

"You may remove your blindfold." Oren wasn't surprised to hear Doug's voice.

After removing his blindfold it took a few seconds for his eyes to adjust to the bright lights. Doug was standing in front of Oren. "Why did you take me here?"

Oren quickly looked around and noticed the driver and the man that blindfolded him were off to his right, and two more of Doug's goons were smoking cigarettes near the door.

Oren panned over to his left and noticed a young girl sitting on a countertop. It was Molly. Oren quickly looked away in disgust.

"Is this where you store the drugs? In this warehouse?" Oren knew right away he asked too many questions and wished he could take his words back.

"It would be wise to keep your mouth shut and just listen," Doug said.

"You have one more business deal with me. Remember?"

Oren nodded. "Yes."

"Now I have a large shipment of cocaine coming in from Colombia," Oren started shaking his head as he knew where this was going.

"And from what I understand, you are going to Colombia with your lovely girlfriend Megan."

Oren was pissed off. "How did you know?"

Doug ignored Oren's question and continued. "And she will have a large shipment of flowers going through the border."

"How the fuck did you know about this?"

"And we are going to hide our shipment of coke within the flowers."

Oren shook his head. "The border guards aren't idiots. They will go through the shipment and find your coke."

"Maybe but I'll take my chances, especially since it will be Megan who will get arrested."

"But you will lose all your money!"

"Look. Her flowers have been going through the border for years. They all know her and trust her. So I highly doubt we'll get caught. You just have to keep it in check."

"What do you mean keep it in check?"

"Oren. You must ensure that this deal goes through."

"I'm not doing this."

"You know that you don't have a choice."

"Yes I do."

"If you don't do this we'll kill both you and your lovely fiancée."

Oren felt sick. "You bugged our house?"

Doug ignored the question and carried on with their conversation.

"When you arrive at El Dorado Airport, you will open up a locker and take the mobile phone."

Doug threw a locker key to Oren and it landed at his feet.

"Now I would keep that key close to your heart. If you lose it the deal won't go through and you know the consequences."

Oren bent over and picked up the key. The number 235 was labelled on it, which was also his apartment number. Oren knew that this was more than a coincidence. It was just Doug's subtle way of controlling him with fear.

"There will be a contact saved in the address book on that mobile and you will call it straight away." Doug took a few steps towards Oren and looked at him intensely in the eyes. "And you will follow the instructions."

Oren didn't say a word.

"Do you understand?" Doug asked.

Oren closed his eyes. "Yes."

Doug clapped his hands together. "Great."

Oren didn't move.

"Now to reward such a great business partner Molly here gives great blow jobs."

That was Molly's cue to jump down from the counter and she walked towards Doug.

"Isn't she a little hottie?"

Oren guessed that Doug sensed his discomfort with such a young prostitute and wanted to torture him even more.

"I don't think so," Oren said.

"You're insulting her," Doug said.

Oren didn't bite. "I would never cheat on my fiancée."

Doug smiled. "It's just a thank you blow job."

Oren raised his voice. "I consider kissing cheating."

"Okay. Your loss," Doug said.

"Are we done?" Oren asked.

"Yes. Like always it's a pleasure doing business with you." Doug winked at Oren, which sent a shiver down his spine. "Blindfold him and take him home."

Doug started to walk away. "Actually, take him to Rose Petal Flowers. Megan is still there and I think she needs some company."

Oren was about to tell Doug to go fuck himself when he felt the bandana cover his eyes. He was then escorted back to the SUV.

Fear and anger were the dominating emotions for the entire drive back to Vancouver. Initially, Oren was thinking of ways to kill Doug; but would stop short when he realised that he didn't even know where he could find him.

When the blindfold was finally removed Oren looked out the window and realised that they were only a few blocks away from Megs' flower shop in Vancouver. They pulled the car over and Oren jumped out. He walked towards Rose Petal Flowers until the SUV was out of sight.

Oren was relieved. Megs wasn't at her shop, she was in her office at the distribution warehouse in South Burnaby. They must not know about the warehouse and Oren wanted to keep it that way. So instead, Oren went home just in case he was being followed.

This time Oren decided to take a taxi. When they finally reached his apartment he looked around and thankfully there were no suspicious vehicles in sight.

It was nearly 3 a.m., but Oren was still wired from the ordeal with Doug. He opened the door and saw Megs' purse. Oren quietly entered the bedroom where Megs was sleeping so peacefully. Oren watched her for a few minutes and decided to take his clothes off and slide into bed next to her. He wrapped his arms around her warm body and kissed her back. The feeling of dread overcame him. "I'm sorry," Oren whispered.

Megs mumbled in her sleep. "I love you, too."

Oren was thankful that she misunderstood what he had said, but then guilt washed over him. He hugged Megs' even tighter.

Chapter 16

The Boeing 737 was on its final approach and Megs was relieved. From the moment that they hopped in their car and drove to Seattle, Oren was complaining. He complained that the long-term parking was too far away from the airport. He complained that the layover in Atlanta was too long. He didn't have one good thing to say about the flight attendants, and even told a mother to control her son because his crying was keeping him awake. This embarrassed Megs so she would apologise to the victims of Oren's wrath when he would go to the washroom.

"C'mon! Hurry up people. You can see that the line is moving so get your bags beforehand," Oren said.

Megs couldn't take it anymore. "Shut up Oren!" She looked around embarrassed, but most of the passengers seemed to be ignoring them.

Megs and Oren didn't say a word to each other until they were through customs and waiting for their luggage.

"It feels like a damn sauna in here. Haven't they ever heard of air conditioning?" Oren said.

"I'm not responding to that dickhead statement," Megs said.

"Can you wait here? I have to take a leak," Oren said.

"Good for you," Megs said.

"Whatever." Oren then walked towards the washroom. He looked back and he noticed Megs sit down beside the conveyor belt messing around with her cell phone. Oren assumed that it would be a while before the ground crew would retrieve the luggage, which suited him fine. He had to sneak away and get the phone in the locker. And it looked like the lockers were in the general direction of the washrooms.

He bypassed the washrooms and began searching for locker 235. When he found it he opened it up and grabbed the phone.

There was only one contact saved on the phone. "Mother," Oren said out loud to himself.

Oren wondered if this was done on purpose, and if Doug knew that his mother was dead. Oren was sure that this was a form of control or a scare tactic. Maybe it's some sort of subliminal message from Doug saying that he'll kill him if he doesn't succeed with the drug trafficking task.

Oren shook that thought from his head and called "Mother".

After 10 rings the phone just hung up. Oren was confused. He was about to call again when the cell phone started ringing.

After a few rings Oren answered the phone. "Hello."

"Tuesday, 1p.m. at La Ponderosa," a man said on the other end of the phone.

"Where is it?" Oren asked.

"Near your hotel." And the man hung up.

Oren put the phone in his pocket and quickly walked back towards the washrooms. He looked over towards Megs, and she was still sitting in the same place messing around with her cell.

When Oren walked back over towards Megs she looked up at him.

"What?" Oren asked.

"I'm waiting for you to complain about the toilets."

Just then the conveyor belt was turned on, which made Megs jump.

"Probably a bad place to sit when this thing is running," Oren said.

Oren smiled at Megs. He knew that he was being a pain in the ass but he was really stressed out.

"How much do you want to bet that our luggage won't turn up?" Oren asked.

"Actually, you pessimistic twat, my luggage gets lost about 50 per cent of the time. But it always shows up a few days later. Did you pack extra clothes in your carry on?"

"No."

Megs smirked. "I didn't think so." And she walked towards the luggage chute. She couldn't stand being near Oren anymore.

*****

Megs and Oren spent the weekend acclimatizing. After a night's sleep Oren wasn't so moody and was much more pleasant to be around. Like every year when Megs visits Bogotá, she hired the same trustworthy driver; and he drove them to various touristy hotspots.

They started off at Plaza Bolivar and took cheesy photos beside a large bronze statue of Simon Bolivar. They were cultured at the Museo Nacional and then later in the evening they boozed it up in the La Candelaria district.

Oren's highlight was their meat fest at Andre Carne de Res. He had a steak the size of his head, and it was cooked to perfection.

"What's wrong Oren?" Megs asked.

"What do mean?"

"You've been kinda distant all day."

"I'm just tired. Maybe a bit jet-lagged. That's all."

Megs didn't look convinced.

Oren put his hand on hers. "Seriously, I'm fine."

Megs smiled and then Oren carried on eating his steak.

Although he was enjoying his time with Megs, he couldn't shake the fear of his meeting on Tuesday with some big drug lord. It shadowed every fun thing he and Megs did together, and she sensed it.

*****

Megs started to get excited as she approached José Gonzalaz's flower farm. It was Monday morning and this was Megs' first work-related meeting. From the car she could see rows of flowers emanating red, orange and yellow that extended out for miles. The roses and carnations were especially magnificent. As they approached the house, José came out to greet his visitors.

Megs looked over to the driver and in Spanish she said. "Would you like come in with us Miguel?"

"Oh no, I have some other errands to run. Call me when you are ready to leave and I will pick you up."

"But Bogotá is nearly an hour away," Megs said.

Miguel smiled which emphasized the laugh lines around his dark eyes. "Oh no. I have some food in the trunk I'm taking to my uncle's place. He doesn't live far from here. I want to spend some time with him."

"Fair enough," Megs said and she waved good-bye as Miguel reversed out of the drive.

"Ola!" Megs said as she approached José and he kissed each side of her cheek.

"This is my fiancé Oren. He doesn't speak very much Spanish," Megs said.

José walked over to Oren and shook his hand. "My Ingles is poco but I will try."

Oren returned the smile. "Me Espanol es poco, too." Megs cringed at Oren's attempt at speaking Spanish.

"Muy bueno," José said to Oren trying to be encouraging.

José's was such a pleasant man and Megs loved working with him. He treated his staff with respect and paid them fairly. Most importantly, he didn't hire anyone under the age of 18, which went against the norm of the many flower farms in Colombia.

"Before work, we must have café," José said and he led Oren and Megs into his house.

José disappeared for a few minutes and returned with his wife. Right away Megs stood up and greeted her.

"Greta! I'm so happy to see you. It's been too long," Megs said in Spanish.

Megs and Greta were about the same height with petite frames. Although Greta's hair was quite straight, Oren thought that she could pass as Megs' older sister.

"Greta, this is my fiancé Oren," Megs said.

"Nice to meet you." Greta's English was a lot better than her husband's.

The four of them sat around the table and drank coffee as Greta updated Megs about the farm, and how much they expanded their flower business in the last year. Oren couldn't keep up with their Spanish conversation so his mind started to wander. Oren kept thinking about the drug cartel and Doug. He looked at José who was also involved with the girls' conversation and would add his two cents every so often. Oren couldn't quite figure out how old José was. He looked about the same age as their driver as he too had quite a few crow's feet around his eyes. José works in the sun all day long so it wasn't a surprise that he was showing signs of advanced aging. Miguel, on the other hand, has been a taxi driver for years. Although, thinking back to everyone he met in the past few days, many Colombian's looked older than their age regardless of what they did for a living. Oren wondered what José and Greta have been through as Colombia's past is quite dark. In comparison to 10 years ago, Colombia was more stable as the drug trade seemed to have migrated north to Mexico, but some conflict still existed.

Everyone stood up and started walking towards the back door.

"Are you coming Oren?" Megs asked.

Oren followed them, and as they passed through the hallway Oren noticed photos of children on the wall.

"Are these your kids?" Oren asked.

Looking at Megs' expression Oren knew right away that he had asked the wrong question.

A very sombre José put his hand on the photo of two boys sitting together on the front porch. "They are in heaven."

"I'm so sorry," Oren said.

Greta intervened. "Please. Let's go outside. I have lots to show you."

Following behind Greta they entered the maze of flowers. Every time that they would bump into a worker Megs would speak to them. Oren couldn't believe how many people they were employing. And the majority of the workforce was made up of women. They seemed happy and it was quite noticeable that they were very loyal to Greta and José.

Oren started wandering on his own along the rows of flowers and stopped at the roses. The smell always reminded him of his mother. She would keep roses in the bathroom of all places while he was growing up. She used to say that it would cover the smell of "boy bums". As a kid Oren thought it was the funniest thing. But not all of his memories that were triggered were happy ones. When Oren's mom was dying of cancer, he made sure that she always had a new bouquet of roses beside her bed. It was against hospital protocol to allow flowers into the rooms as they believed that it could instigate allergies from the other patients. But in palliative care all those rules were thrown out the window.

Oren closed his eyes and thought about his mom's soft skin and her stern blue eyes. However, her face started to twist and turn as it morphed into somebody else. Oren quickly opened his eyes and he felt sick. Although his mother's stern blue eyes were the same, it was the face of Doug that it morphed into. He couldn't shake the image from his head. Oren quickly walked back and went straight into the house quickly looking for the bathroom. When he found it he started to throw up in the toilet. Oren recalled Megs' conversation with Greta when they were drinking coffee not even 30 minutes prior. He was certain that they planned to send another shipment by the end of this week to Vancouver.

"Was this the shipment that Doug planned to plant the cocaine?" Oren asked himself.

Oren's mind was going in circles. If they got caught at the airport it wasn't only Megs and him who were going down, it would be José and Greta, too. The whole farm and its workers could potentially be thrown in jail.

Oren rinsed his face and looked at himself in the mirror. Just then it dawned on him that jail would be the desired alternative. If they got busted then the drug cartels would potentially kill them all. And this was the main reason that he cannot fail.

"You alright Oren?" Megs said as she knocked on the bathroom door.

"Yeah. I just had to go to the bathroom," Oren said.

"Well I hope you're hungry because Greta is making us lunch," Megs said.

Oren wasn't hungry, but he knew he had to keep it together and try hard to act normal as possible.

"Great. I'll be out in a minute," Oren said.

Oren wiped his face with a hand towel and went into the kitchen.

As Oren entered the kitchen he bumped into Greta who was rushing around putting together some food for the four of them.

"Do you need any help?" Oren asked.

"Oh no. They are outside at the table talking. You should go, too." Although Greta smiled, Oren could see much pain in her eyes. He assumed that he triggered some sad memories when he asked about her sons.

Oren joined José and Megs outside and there was a pitcher of sangria on the table.

"Sangria? Or Cervesa?" José asked.

"Sangria is fine. Muchas gracias," Oren said.

Oren placed his hand on Megs' leg and smiled at her and they continued with their conversation, which was inevitably about the business.

Oren felt that José and Greta were great people who have had enough tragedy in their life. Oren would have loved to change the situation, but it was out of his control. Doug hijacked Megs' flower business to use it for a much darker purpose, and all Oren could do was ensure that it succeeded and ran smoothly. This was the first time things were out of Oren's control, and it both frightened him and infuriated him.

Greta came out with some cured meat and bread and plonked it on the middle of the table.

"Tomorrow I promise I will make bandeja paisa," Greta said.

Oren was surprised. "Tomorrow?"

Megs was confused with Oren's reaction. "Yeah, I told you that I need to spend a couple of days here at the very least. We have so much to do."

Greta and José nodded in agreement.

Oren's face went red. "Oh no. That's not what I meant. I just feel a bit in the way."

"Of course you're not in the way babes. And I promise there won't be so much shop talk tomorrow," Megs said.

Oren's heart sunk. He would have to think of a way to get out of coming to José and Greta's farm tomorrow.

*****

Oren abruptly woke up to the sound of Megs' alarm on her cell phone. He barely slept all night and kept waking up every hour.

"Jesus Christ, I hate your fucking alarm," Oren said before putting his pillow over his head.

"Good morning to you, too, asshole," Megs said.

She abruptly got up and went into the bathroom slamming the door behind her.

Oren knew that he went too far, but he was in a terrible mood.

Oren walked into the bathroom. "Look. I'm sorry. I barely slept last night."

"Do you mind? I'm peeing."

"I just don't understand why you have to have a foghorn as your alarm sound."

"It's not a foghorn. It's the sound of the ocean. It turns into a foghorn if I don't turn off the alarm right away."

"Okay. Whatever."

"My alarm that you have never complained about before by-the-way is much better than you swearing at me."

"I didn't swear at you. I swore at the situation."

"Because I set my alarm? I have to work today. This isn't a holiday."

"Oh my god this conversation is going nowhere. I'm sorry Megs. I shouldn't have snapped at you, but I slept like shit last night."

"Well, I don't deserve the f-bomb."

"I didn't give you the f-bomb. I gave it to your alarm."

Megs got up from the toilet and turned on the shower.

"Are you taking a shower, too? We don't have much time before we have to leave. Miguel will be here soon."

"I feel like shit Megs. I barely slept last night and my head is throbbing."

"It's your fault. You didn't have to get drunk last night."

"Sorry Megs. I'm not going. I don't feel good."

Oren left the bathroom and went back to bed.

Once Megs was out of the shower she left the bathroom and sat on the bed with a towel around her.

"I was thinking. Do you feel bad about the kid thing yesterday?" Megs said.

Oren wasn't sure how to answer that question so he let Megs continue.

"As I said last night I'm very sorry that I didn't tell you about their sons. It's an awful tragedy that is still fairly new. It's only my second time seeing Greta and José after their sons' death."

Megs' eyes started to tear up as she continued talking. "I hate the fucking drug cartel. So much death and destruction. Actually, I don't know who I hate more. Those who buy that white shit or the ones trafficking it."

Megs grabbed a tissue on the nightstand and blew her nose.

"If there was no more demand there would be no more supply. Fucking rich Westerners and their goddamn glamour drug."

By the minute Megs was making Oren feel worse than he already did, so he finally interrupted her. "Look. I'm sorry Megs. I don't want to come today. It's everything. I don't feel good. I feel horrible about making Greta and José feel bad...."

"Okay. I get your point. Fair enough. I shouldn't be too late tonight. And if you need anything call me."

Megs got up and started to get dressed.

Oren got out of bed and walked over to Megs. He hugged her from behind and started to kiss her neck. "I'm so sorry beautiful. I'll make it up to you tonight. I promise."

Megs smiled. "You so owe me."

Megs' cell phone started ringing. "Oh shit, it's Miguel. I think he's the only Colombian who is always early."

Megs kissed Oren and ran out of the hotel room.

Before going back to bed Oren popped a couple of ibuprofen tablets. He wanted to be in full form during his meeting with "Mother" that afternoon.

*****

Oren was about 10 minutes early when he walked into Ponderosa's. He quickly scanned the room noticing two small families, three couples, a middle-age man with a briefcase who looked like a lawyer, and a lady with dyed blond hair who was on her cell phone. He couldn't see anyone who may look like a drug dealer anywhere in the restaurant, so he sat himself at a table facing the door. The waitress came over and put a menu on his table. She proceeded to speak to him in Spanish and the only word he was able to recognise was "bebida".

Oren looked up at the waitress. "Ahhh....para mis un vino tino por favor."

The waitress smiled and said "si senor". Oren was expecting her to ask what type of wine he wanted, but she quickly walked away. About a minute later she walked over and showed him two bottles of wine, which were both from Chile.

"Quanto es?" Oren asked.

"Two US dollars," the waitress replied.

"For the entire bottle?" Oren said.

The waitress started laughing and shook her head. "One glass."

"Okay. I'll take that one." Oren pointed at the bottle on his left. He didn't recognise either of the bottles, but his experience with Chilean wine tended to be very good.

The waitress poured him a glass and said something quickly in Spanish.

Oren thought perhaps she was asking if he wanted some food.

"I just need to read the menu first."

At first the waitress didn't understand and asked another question.

Oren smiled and pointed at his eyes and then the menu. "Uno memento, I need to read the menu first."

The waitress started laughing and patted him on the back, then walked away.

Oren wasn't sure what he said that was so funny but at least he wasn't offensive, which he had a habit of doing since arriving in Colombia. So he just shook his head and started reading the menu.

Oren wasn't even on the second page when a shadow appeared over his table. Someone was hovering over top of him and it wasn't the waitress. Oren's heart started racing and he looked up. To his surprise the man who Oren thought was a lawyer was standing over top of him.

"Do you mind if I join you?" Right away Oren recognised the voice. It was the same man that Oren spoke to who was known as Mother.

Oren nodded and Mother sat down.

"I recommend the tortillas," Mother said.

Oren smiled and closed his menu. Although it was quite obvious that Mother comes from a Spanish-speaking country, his grasp on the English language was perfect. Oren was certain that he was educated.

Oren didn't even notice when the waitress walked over as he was startled when she spoke to Mother in Spanish. They went back and forth, and she jotted a few things down on her note pad and walked away.

"I just ordered you some tortillas." Mother studied Oren for a few seconds before he carried on talking. "You don't know much Spanish do you?"

Oren's heart rate was nearly back to normal. "Poco."

"I just thought with a Puerto Rican girlfriend you would have made more of an effort," Mother said.

Oren felt his face flush. "How do you know that my girlfriend is Puerto Rican?"

"Doug knows everything. He studied you a lot before making the decision of asking you to be his business partner. He's a very careful man."

"Business partner?" Oren shook his head and learned over the table towards Mother. "I didn't exactly have a choice."

"Calm down. You are making a scene. I think it's pretty obvious that I'm only Doug's lawyer."

Oren couldn't help but laugh at that idea. It was obvious that he was more than a lawyer, but he played the part very well.

Oren sat back and tried his best to relax. "What is the plan?"

Just then the waitress came over and put the plates in front of the two men. Oren wasn't feeling particularly hungry, but he decided to eat so that they didn't look any more suspicious than they already did in the restaurant.

Once the waitress was out of ear shot Mother spoke. "All you have to do is tell me when the shipment is leaving Gonzalaz's farm."

Oren hesitated, but he knew everyone's lives were upon his shoulders so he had to ensure that the drug deal was successful. "Yesterday I overheard Megs say later this week. She didn't mention an exact date."

Although the drug cartel knew everything about Megs anyways, Oren felt extremely uncomfortable saying her name out loud.

"In other words, it could be Thursday or Friday?" Mother said.

"Yeah. I guess so," Oren replied.

Mother looked intensely into Oren's eyes. "I need an exact date."

"Look, I don't have it yet. Megs is at the Gonzalaz's farm today, so I'm assuming that is one of the topics they are currently discussing."

"All you must tell me is the time the flower shipment is being picked up and what flight it will be on. My men can figure everything else out in between."

Oren nodded in agreement.

"You must give us at least 24 hours so my men can organise this."

Mother stared at Oren looking for a response.

"Okay," Oren finally said.

"If you don't give us a 24-hour notice there will be serious consequences."

Oren didn't say a word and just when the silence between the two men became unbearable, Mother finally continued. "Do you understand?"

"Yes," Oren said.

Mother picked up his briefcase and stood up. He threw a handful of Colombian pesos on the table and looked at Oren and smiled. "I look forward to your call."

Oren didn't move for a few minutes after Mother left, and his thoughts were only interrupted when the waitress started to clear off the table.

Oren tried his best to smile. "Gracias." And he left Ponderosa's heading straight to his hotel room.

As soon as Oren entered the room he ran to the bathroom and started to vomit in the toilet. As he flushed, he watched the remnants of the tortilla and red wine spin around in circles before being sucked into the hotel's shitty plumbing system. Oren washed his face and rinsed out his mouth as the taste of vomit was more vile than usual. He felt like he just completed a deal with the devil. He looked at himself in the mirror and didn't recognise the man that stared back at him. This other Oren looked haggard, old and the circles around his eyes were darker than usual. It felt like an eternity went by since he last slept through an entire night.

Oren walked over to the bed and collapsed on top of the duvet. His head wasn't even on the pillow, but he didn't care. He just stared at the ceiling. It didn't take long before fatigue overcame him and he closed his eyes.

*****

"Tomorrow you'll be dead!" Straight away Oren recognised Mother's voice. Initially he was startled, but after a few seconds he realised that it was only a dream; so he cleared his mind and relaxed back into the Land of Nod.

"Tomorrow you'll be dead!" Oren felt the warmth of someone's breath on his face and he forced himself awake.

"Get up sleepy head!" Megs was hovering over top of Oren.

"Jesus, Megs. You startled me."

"Sorry babe, but I've been back for nearly an hour now and I'm hungry."

"Shit. Sorry. I didn't realise that I was out that long."

"Are you feeling better now?"

"Yeah, I am."

"Great! Because tomorrow we're going to the Savanna."

"What?"

"I'm meeting with another farmer tomorrow. He's José and Greta's friend, and is looking for a partnership with a North American company. So I've agreed to meet with him."

Megs looked at Oren. "What's wrong?"

"Oh nothing, I just thought we were basing ourselves here."

"Savanna of Bogotá is beautiful. It's up in the Andes so it's a bit of a trek. I thought you wanted to see the mountains?"

Oren didn't know why he was so worried about leaving Bogotá as he only needed to call Mother once he knew the flower shipment details. So it didn't matter where he was based. He was relieved at this revelation and hugged Megs.

"No no. I'm really excited. I thought I'd get a few more days to acclimatize, that's all. I've just been feeling ill and I wasn't expecting this."

"I'm sorry. I only found out about this today, and with my schedule it's the only time I can fit it in."

Oren kissed Megs on her forehead and worked his way down to her mouth.

Megs pushed Oren away and started laughing. "You have really bad doggy breath."

Oren smiled. "Gimme a break. I just woke up and I was probably mouth breathing again."

"You weren't exactly Sleeping Beauty!"

Oren got up. "I just need a few minutes to get ready and I'm taking you out."

Megs looked excited. "Where?"

"It's a surprise. This morning I promised that I'll make it up to you."

In reality Oren had no clue where he was taking Megs, but he had about 10 minutes to figure something out while he was showering.

Chapter 17

While Oren and Megs were in Colombia, Claire decided to spend more time at her actual clinic. The morning was insanely busy and Claire didn't take her lunch until 2 o'clock. One of the nurses actually ordered her to take a half hour break. Claire was about halfway through her burrito when there was a knock at the door.

"Dr. Lalonde. A Dr. Wu is here to see you."

"Sure. Let him in," Claire said.

As soon as Terry walked into her office she could see that something was wrong. He closed the door and handed her the newspaper, which he was carrying in his hand.

"Harley Knowle. Do you remember him?" Terry asked.

"Yeah. He's the guy that misled the cops for us," Claire said.

"He was also one of Oren's main clients outside of the drug cartel," Terry said.

Claire wasn't sure where Terry was going with this. "Can you just tell me what's going on?"

"He's dead, Claire. His obituary is in today's newspaper."

Claire looked down at the newspaper and read the article. "Okay. Harley's dead. Are you insinuating that we go to his funeral or something?"

Terry sat down and looked intensely into Claire's eyes. "Don't you get it Claire? What if they find our fake and very illegal prescriptions in his home?"

"You are being paranoid Terry." Claire finished her burrito and gave the newspaper back to Terry. "And I don't think his loved ones are really going to notice any potentially suspicious prescriptions."

"What about the cops?" Terry asked.

"Why would the cops be there?"

147

"Because his death is deemed suspicious. He overdosed on narcotics Claire. And there was enough evidence in his room to trace it back to us!"

"How the hell do you know that?"

"After I read his obituary, I went on the internet and there's an article stating that a man was found dead and it may be due to an overdose."

Claire started searching for this article on the internet. "This article ran over a week ago."

Terry cut Claire off and continued talking. "For obvious reasons I wanted to find out more, so I called a good friend of mine who works as an orderly at the same hospital where they performed the autopsy. And it looks like he overdosed on fentanyl. Apparently he extracted the drug out of the patch, heated it up and injected it."

Claire was shocked. "What a fucking idiot. I know for a fact that Oren warned him about the strength of fentanyl. Taking that much all at once is suicidal!"

Terry shook his head. "Harley Knowle was too arrogant to kill himself. So he was either seriously addicted or someone else injected it."

Claire knew exactly where Terry was going with this. "You think that Doug has something to do with this?"

"I don't know. But his house was cordoned off for too long to be just an overdose. From what his neighbours were telling me the cops were there for days following his death. I think something else is up."

"You certainly have been doing lots of sleuthing," Claire said.

"Thank god we kept record of our client's addresses." Terry looked away from Claire. "I'm just trying to cover our asses. Remember that I've got a kid, too."

Claire could see tears welling up in Terry's eyes. "What are we going to do?"

"We need to call Oren." Claire picked up her cell.

"I've already tried that Claire. It's going directly to his voice mail," Terry said.

Claire ignored Terry and still tried phoning him. "Hey Oren. I hope you and Megs are having a wonderful time in Colombia, but I need you to call me back ASAP." Claire was worried about Megs hearing the message so she didn't mention Harley.

Claire was annoyed. "Do cell phones even exist in Colombia? Oren said we will be able to reach him!"

"He's probably just in an area where there's no signal. I'm sure he'd have signal in Bogotá," Terry said.

They sat in silence for a few minutes and an idea came to Claire.

"Remember Detective Mazis?" Claire asked.

"The Mulder lookalike?"

"I fucked him."

"Thanks for sharing Claire."

"What I mean is that perhaps I can meet up with him again. He's one of the main detectives in the Drug Unit. So he must know about Harley."

"How are you going to extract that information from him?" Terry stood up. "Actually, I don't want to know. Just do what you have to do."

"Stay away from the homeopathic clinic until I find out more," Claire said.

"I got to go. I'm picking up Ethan from school soon."

"Seriously Terry. It's going to be okay. We're probably just being paranoid."

Terry smiled at Claire and left her office.

Claire had a few more hours left of her shift, which she had no choice but to finish. She couldn't stop thinking about her conversation with Terry. Her mind was running in circles. She didn't even know how to approach Evan since they haven't spoken to each other since Claire abruptly left his house. "This is going to be so awkward," Claire said to herself.

*****

After work Claire drove directly to Evan's house, but there were no cars in the drive. Even if he was there she wouldn't dare knock on the door. Claire didn't want to see neither his wife nor his children. It would hurt too much. Claire decided it would be easier to meet with him at work. She opened up her purse and took Evan's business card out. Unfortunately, it just had a direct line and his email address. Claire needed to see him in person straight away as she couldn't risk him ignoring her. She assumed that he would be based at VPD's Headquarters on Cambie Street and decided to drive straight there.

As Claire approached VPD's parking lot she started to get quite nervous as hardly any thought went into how to approach Evan. Claire sat in her car for a few minutes as she gathered enough courage to go into the building. She took a couple of deep breaths, grabbed her purse and got out of the car. Claire then confidently walked into VPD's HQ building.

Although Claire was quite the deviant growing up, she had never been in the police station before. Claire approached the front desk. "Hi. I'm looking for a Detective Evan Mazis. He's with the Drug Unit." Claire shrugged her shoulders and smiled. "I don't even know if he's in this building. All he gave me was his business card with a phone number and email address." Claire showed the security guard, who was behind the desk, the business card.

"Why didn't you just call him?" The security guard asked.

"Because I need to speak with him in person. It's urgent. I have more information." The security guard stopped Claire midsentence.

"I'm assuming that this in confidential. Let me call his office." The security guard picked up the phone.

"Is Detective Mazis there?"

Claire's heart was pounding fast as she thought about her encounter with Evan.

"Thanks." And the security guard hung up the phone.

"He's out on the field. You should probably try calling him."

Claire nodded and smiled at the security guard. She turned around and started to walk out of the building. As Claire approached the door, to her surprise, Evan and three other police officers were walking in. Since Detective Simpson wasn't there Claire quickly changed her planned approach.

Evan looked even more surprised than Claire. "Oh! Dr. Lalonde. How can I help you?"

"Detective Mazis, I really need to talk to you. It's about your interview with me at my clinic concerning drug trafficking."

Evan jumped in before Claire could say anything else as the case was confidential. "Okay okay. Please come into my office. You have to clear security first." And Evan escorted Claire through the metal detectors and waited for her on the other side as security went through her bags.

Claire followed Evan through what seemed like a maze before reaching his office.

"Take a seat Claire," Evan said and he shut the door.

"I'm not here about the drug trafficking thing," Claire said.

"Then what are you here for?" Evan asked.

"Just give me two minutes of your time," Claire said.

Evan looked confused.

"I couldn't call you because I was afraid that you would hang up. And I didn't feel comfortable going to your house for obvious reasons. So this is the only way I could see you again."

"Claire. You were very clear that you didn't want to see me again."

"But for some strange reason I feel so bad about....about everything," Claire started welling up. "I basically left you with your dick in your hand."

"Eloquently put," Evan said.

Claire interrupted him and continued. "I shouldn't have handled it that way. I was very childish."

Evan passed a couple of tissues to Claire.

"I am genuinely confused here Claire. I was the asshole who was cheating on his wife and I lied to you about it."

"I know but..."

"And to be honest with you, I'm absolutely flabbergasted that you are here feeling bad."

Evan put his hand on Claire's. "I'm the one who should be apologising. Not you."

With her free hand Claire wiped her eyes with the tissue.

"Look. How about we talk about this more after my shift. I have some paperwork to do, but how about we meet at 8 p.m."

Claire smiled. "Okay. That would be nice."

"Have you been to Six Acres before?" Evan asked.

"It's in Gastown, right?" Claire said.

"Yes. On the corner of Carrall Street." Evan got up to escort Claire back through the building.

"Is my mascara running?" Claire asked.

"No. You look beautiful," Evan said.

Claire smiled and followed Evan through the corridors and down a few floor in the elevator finally making it to the exit.

Claire quickly left the building and hopped into her car.

"I should win a fucking Grammy for that." Claire said to herself as she looked in the rear view mirror. She cleaned the smudged black mascara below her eyes and quickly drove off.

*****

Claire was about 30 minutes early when she arrived at the bar. Six Acres was always busy, and she wanted to ensure they got a somewhat private table on the second floor. Luckily she didn't have to wait that long, and was seated near the washrooms at a table for two. Claire ordered a glass of wine to calm her nerves.

Claire wanted to look respectable rather than seductive as this was not a date. So Claire chose to wear her skinny jeans and a loose long shirt that covered her bum so not to give the wrong impression. Screwing a married man was not on her to-do list. However, extracting important information was. She still wasn't sure how she was going to approach the Harley overdosing subject, but decided it would only be safe after Evan had a couple of drinks when he loosened up a bit.

Claire looked at her watch and noticed that it was 8:05 already and she had drunk half of her glass of wine. She needed to be careful not to drink too much in order to stay alert, so she ordered a glass of water.

Claire looked at her cell phone again and it was 8:15. Claire started to worry that Evan wasn't going to show up.

Just as Claire started to fear that Evan would be a no-show he came clomping up the stairs behind a waiter. "I'm so sorry Claire. A couple of hobos were fighting a few blocks from here, so I tried to separate them. I ended up phoning the cops and had to wait until they got there. Gastown is such a colourful area."

Claire started laughing. "Hobos? I can't remember the last time I heard anyone use that word."

Evan smiled. "They must have been in their 60s and they had long beards. To me that's a hobo. It was actually quite the scene."

"What were they fighting about?" Claire asked.

"It's hard to say. I think one was accusing the other of stealing from their grocery cart. It was full of junk!"

"That junk is their worldly possessions," Claire said.

"I know. I must seem so insensitive."

Claire wasn't sure if Evan was being sarcastic or not, but she wasn't going to press the issue.

"What can I get ya?" a waiter asked.

Evan looked up. "Whatever hoppy beer you have on draught."

"Good thing we only have one." The waiter smiled and walked away.

"So did you finish all your paperwork?" Claire asked.

"Screw this small talk Claire. You probably want to know what's going on with me and my wife. Right?"

Truthfully Claire didn't give a shit, but she had to carry on her act in order to get any information about Harley. "Well, yeah, I guess. But please don't say anything if you feel that it is too personal."

"I'm a sex addict," Evan said just as the waiter put his pint of beer on the table.

Claire couldn't help herself and started giggling.

Evan glared at the waiter and he walked away, but she could see that he was laughing too even though his back was facing them.

"What's so funny? This is serious Claire."

"I'm sorry. I just wasn't expecting you to say that."

"My shrink officially diagnosed me with that disorder. It's hard to believe, eh?"

"Well, come to think of it, sex addiction goes hand-in-hand with OCD, narcissistic personality disorder."

Evan interrupted and was clearly offended. "Are you saying that I'm a narcissist?"

Claire had to think fast. "I didn't mean it like that. I don't even know you well enough to diagnose you with anything. It's just that a lot of cops, especially in your high position, tend to be slightly narcissistic."

"Well, I don't consider myself a narcissist, but I do suffer from OCD."

Claire was about to say that narcissist generally don't admit that they are, but decided it would be best not to get in a heated debate with Evan as it could go very wrong.

"Does your wife know about this?" Claire asked.

"After you flipped out on me and made me feel horrible about myself, I told her that I cheated on her because she isn't giving me enough sex."

Claire couldn't contain her anger. "That's awful Evan!"

"Shhh...calm down." Evan downed nearly half his pint.

"I told her that I think I have a problem and that I wanted to see a therapist."

"And she agreed?" Claire asked.

"Absolutely, I think that statement could possibly save our marriage. I do love her Claire, but we have sex about once a month if I'm lucky."

"Oh my god." Claire couldn't imagine going a month without sex and started to see it from Evan's point of view.

"This has been ongoing for years. So she agreed to go to a therapist with me."

Evan finished his beer and waved the waiter over. "Could I have another one please? And it looks like the lady needs a top up, too."

Claire looked down at her glass and it was about a quarter full. So she drank what was remaining of her wine and gave the empty glass to the waiter.

"How are the sessions going?" Claire asked.

"They are fine, but we agreed to separate for a few weeks. I'm staying at the Holiday Inn on Howe Street. I miss my family, but apparently this is supposed to make things better. The shrink suggested it."

"Well, it certainly sounds like you are suffering from sexual frustration rather than sex addiction Evan."

"I left out an important fact. The shrink also suggested that we see him individually. And he asked me how many times I really cheated on my wife. He totally knew that I underestimated big time. I just couldn't be honest with my wife on the numbers. That's when he told me that I was addicted to sex, and perhaps by putting pressure on my wife to have sex all the time actually pushed her away."

"Wow. Now that's fucked up," Claire said.

"And I have been living in the Holiday Inn for just over a week now and I am proud to say that I haven't had sex."

"And you won't be starting with me." Instantly Claire regretted that she said that. "I'm so sorry Evan. I just don't want to get in between you and your wife. I didn't mean to sound so rude."

"No. This is a test. Right now I want to desperately have sex with you, but I know that I can't. And I can assure you, Claire, it's really goddamn hard. But I am here as a friend without benefits."

Claire smiled. "Okay. Let's shake on it."

Claire and Evan shook hands.

"I have to change the subject," Evan said and looked around. "Where the hell is my beer?"

Claire could see the waiter walking up the stairs with a tray full of drinks. "Don't worry, it's coming."

Once the waiter was out of earshot Evan leaned towards Claire. "I have to ask you a serious question. Do you know where Oren is? I've been trying to get a hold of him for a few days."

Claire's heart dropped. "He's in Colombia with his fiancé. They probably don't have signal."

"Why do you look so worried Claire?" Evan asked.

"Because a detective is asking where my friend is in a serious cop-like voice."

Evan started laughing. "I just have a few questions about one of his patients."

"He could be one of mine as well. We don't have strict patients for each doctor. It's really who is available at the time."

Evan shrugged his shoulders. "My partner and I had a chat with Harley Knowle who was acting quite suspicious when he left your clinic a few months ago. Recently he was found dead in his apartment."

Claire tried her best to act surprised. "Was he murdered or something? What the hell does this have to do with us?"

"Calm down Claire. His death wasn't deemed suspicious as it was pretty clear that he overdosed, but the amount of illegal narcotics that were found in his apartment was enough to raise suspicion."

Claire felt like she was going to be sick. "Illegal narcotics?"

"These types of guys have a habit of going from doctor to doctor trying to obtain prescriptions for painkillers of all sorts. It looks like his luck ran out and he had to turn to a proper drug dealer. It's normal protocol to interview as many people as possible to paint a picture of this guy. I'm hoping we can find a lead so that we can nail the big fish."

Claire knew exactly who the big fish was: Doug. But she didn't dare drop his name.

"So do you know anything about Harley?" Evan asked.

"Unfortunately you are right. Oren was the only one who saw him. But I doubt he'll have much to say about him. We see so many patients on a daily basis."

"Well, we are interviewing all of his doctors which will include Oren."

"Fair enough. How were you able to locate all of his doctors?" Claire asked.

Evan slammed back his beer and it was apparent that he was wasted. That last beer just tipped him over the edge.

"Were you drinking before you got here Evan?"

"What? Of course not!" Evan said.

Claire had a sneaky suspicion that he went out with the boys after work before meeting up with her. Claire assumed that he was having a rough time with his family issues that he turned to alcohol. Evan being so opened about the Harley case was making more sense. He was drunk and Claire was about to take advantage of it.

Claire ordered Evan another beer, and ordered a sausage board with extra bread to help soak up some of the booze. She didn't want Evan passing out before she could extract all the information that she needed.

Evan got up and went to the washroom. After about 15 minutes Claire decided to knock on the door. "Are you okay Evan?"

There was no answer so Claire started banging louder.

Evan opened up the door smiled and followed Claire back to their table.

"Sorry Claire. I'm just really tired."

"Have some of my water," Claire said.

Evan thanked Claire and drank the entire glass.

"So where were we?" Evan asked.

"I was just wondering how you were able to figure out who Harley's doctors were?"

Evan looked suspiciously at Claire. "Why do you ask?"

"Well, the only reason why you knew of Oren was because you bumped into Harley at our clinic." Claire put her glass of wine down on the table. "Look, forget it. I know I'm asking too many questions. I just find this investigation stuff fascinating. You cops seem to know what you're doing."

Claire was hoping that her compliment would encourage Evan to speak proudly of his work and share his brilliance. *Such a typical narcissistic trait.* She thought to herself.

Evan grabbed his beer. "I didn't know I ordered another one."

"I did," Claire said.

"Trying to get me drunk, eh?" Evan winked at Claire.

Claire smiled and thought to herself. *The idiot thinks I want to fuck him.*

"In your dreams! I ordered some food and the waiter asked me if you wanted another. I assumed yes."

"Good assumption."

Claire could see the waiter walking up the stairs with their platter.

Evan winked at Claire. "Sausage platter? I think I'm getting your message."

Claire felt like decking him, but she smiled instead.

"I'm not a big fan of pig sausage. These are actually beef."

Evan shook his head and plunged his fork into one of the sliced sausages and then shoved it into his mouth.

"Nope. Tastes like pig to me!"

Claire rolled her eyes and started eating from the platter. She wasn't exactly hungry, but she thought eating would prevent her from becoming too drunk.

After a few minutes of silence finally Evan spoke.

"Don't be fooled. There isn't any special investigation techniques involved with finding Harley's doctors. The forensic team found a whole load of empty pill bottles. I'm talking about suitcases full."

"Holy shit!" Claire said.

Evan shrugged his shoulders. "I don't know if he was too lazy to throw them out or if he was hoarding them for some strange mentally ill reason, but my team is going through them as we speak."

Claire felt sick. She was sure that Oren's pseudo-prescriptions were also left in Harley's apartment.

"Well this is certainly shocking. As doctors we are trained to see these types of individuals. Harley must have been a very good actor."

"Ha! This happens more than you think!" Evan said.

"Really? Well, how many doctors has he tricked so far?"

"Hundreds. All across Canada. He was a truck driver, remember."

"Sounds like your team have their hands full."

"Well, we are working around the clock. I even have unpaid interns working for me right now."

At that point Claire had heard enough. She believed that they didn't find Oren's prescription yet, but soon they would. It could be tonight, tomorrow or next week, but she must assume the worst-case scenario.

"I have to piss," Claire said.

"I thought only guys say that," Evan said.

"I also stand up when I pee," Claire said.

Claire started dialling Oren's phone number when she was in the washroom. Once again, it went straight to his voice mail.

"Fuck!" Claire said.

She then called Terry but only got his voice mail.

"Hi Terry. I know it's late, but I need to talk to you ASAP."

Claire hung up and waited a few more seconds before trying to call Terry again.

"Stupid voice mail," Claire said to herself.

She took a few seconds to calm down and left the washroom.

160

To her surprise there were two waiters telling Evan to leave.

"What's going on here?" Claire asked.

Just then Claire could smell vomit and she looked down.

"Oh my god, I'm so sorry!" Claire said.

"Get him the hell out of here or we're going to call the cops," one of the waiters said.

"I am the cops!" Evan said.

One of the waiters started laughing. "Yeah right buddy."

Claire glared at the waiter as she helped Evan up from his chair.

"C'mon Evan. Let's get out of here."

"Are you going to pay the bill lady?"

"First of all. Don't call me lady. It's rude. And secondly..."

Evan grabbed his wallet out of his back pocket and threw a $100 bill on the table. "Take it and shut the fuck up!"

Just then Claire realised that the entire restaurant was staring at them.

Claire started pulling on Evan. "Please, let's just go." And she dragged him out of the restaurant.

Claire and Evan walked down Water Street and hailed the first taxi they saw.

"Would you like this one?" Evan asked.

"I'll escort you home," Claire said.

"I may be drunk, but I can manage."

"Please take it. You need it more than me."

Before Evan could argue, Claire shut the passenger door and started to walk off.

Once Evan's taxi was out of site, Claire hailed down another. She desperately needed to see Terry.

Claire tried calling Terry's cell six more times as they were driving to his apartment.

"Can you wait out here for a minute?" Claire asked the taxi driver.

Claire buzzed Terry's apartment and after a few rings he answered. "It's Claire. I desperately need to talk to you!"

"Just a second, I'll buzz you in."

"I have to pay the taxi driver. I'll be right back."

Claire ran back over to the taxi. "Call it $15." "Thanks." Claire gave him $20 and ran back to the apartment.

Terry let Claire in.

"I guess you saw Detective Mazis."

"Is Ethan here?"

"No. He's with his mother tonight."

"Good." Claire and Terry sat on the couch facing each other.

"I don't know where to begin."

"Let me get you some water."

"No. Just listen. The cops will soon find Oren's prescriptions. Harley kept them all."

"What do you mean all?"

"It looks like he never threw any of them out. There are hundreds of them!"

"How do you know Oren is one of them?"

"Evan's team is going through them right now. It's only a matter of time before they stumbled on Dr. O'Brian's, which is going to lead them straight to our clinic."

Terry looked extremely worried. "And we can't even play dumb and say that we didn't know. We're a goddamn homeopathic clinic!"

"I know! We're fucked!" Claire said.

After a few minutes Terry finally broke the silence. "Okay. Let's think about this rationally. What could they find in our clinic that would put us in jail?"

"Well, Oren's already screwed," Claire said.

"Our files. And we have hundreds of them," Terry said.

"What about any traces of drugs?" Claire asked.

"You mean Doug's drugs?" Terry asked.

"Would they find any clues that would link us to Doug?"

"Here's a better question Claire. Doug will inevitably find out that our clinic is being investigated. Would he get rid of us?"

Tears started to well up in Claire's eyes. "I'm certain that he will kill us. Of course he fucking will. He can't risk us saying anything to the police. We're disposable!"

Terry hugged Claire. "We will figure something out Claire. If that is the case, perhaps we need to ask for police protection."

After a few minutes being comforted by Terry an idea sprung into Claire's head. "What if we destroy the clinic?"

Terry released the hug and looked at Claire. "Go on."

"If we set it on fire then all of the evidence will be destroyed."

"Do you know enough about fires to make it look accidental? I don't want to turn this into an insurance scam."

"I'd rather deal with an insurance scam than death, Terry."

"I agree."

"How about we pin it on the Anti-Gentrification Front?"

"Isn't their focus more in Downtown Eastside?"

"A few weeks ago they burned down a half constructed condo development just down the road. Their protests are spreading out as far as East Van. Our yuppie holistic clinic is geared towards the rich. If I were them I'd burn us down, too!"

"Are you confident that we can do this?"

"Yes. And we have to do this tonight. They may find one of Oren's prescriptions tomorrow."

"Slow down Claire. Think about what we need."

"A couple of gas cans and some spray paint. That's all they used."

Claire stood up. "I'll meet you a few blocks down from our clinic at 3 a.m. Do you have a gas can?"

Although Terry looked uncomfortable with this plan he nodded yes.

"Perfect!" Claire said and she left his apartment.

Chapter 18

"You told me that I'd get signal up here," Oren said.

"You can. It's just intermittent," Megs said.

"Well, I haven't had any signal on my phone for hours," Oren said.

"We're in a car constantly on the move Oren. You haven't been staring at your stupid cell every minute."

Megs rolled her eyes and stared out the window. Her anger grew towards Oren.

"You've been such a pain in the ass since we landed in Colombia. I'm beginning to regret asking you to come."

"Don't be like that Megs."

"And why are you so obsessed with your cell. You're supposed to be on holiday."

"My patients....whatever Megs. You wouldn't understand."

"Anyways, I'm the one who needs a signal the most."

Oren took advantage of the opportunity to pry about the shipment.

"What for? To sort out the shipment details with José and Greta?"

Megs shook her head. "Of course not. That was organised yesterday."

"Oh," Oren said.

"If we are late or get lost or something I have to call Pedro."

"Who's Pedro?" Oren asked.

"Potentially he's my new partner. That's the farmer who we're meeting. I told you that already."

"What's with the sass? You didn't tell me his name. I'm not a fucking psychic."

Miguel started laughing. "Me estás recordando por qué estoy divorciado."

"What did he just say?" Oren asked.

Megs smiled. "We're reminding him why he's divorced."

"And we're not even married yet," Oren said.

Megs turned away from Oren. "There's still time to back out."

"Oh c'mon Megs, it's just a silly fight."

For nearly an hour they all sat in the car in silence. Oren glanced at his phone and noticed that he had a couple of bars worth of signal.

"You alright Megs? You're awfully quiet."

Megs shrugged her shoulders.

"So are we going to help Greta and José pick the flowers and organise the shipment with them?" Oren asked.

"No, we organised that yesterday. It needs to be on the Saturday evening flight to Toronto."

"That's three days away," Oren said.

"It needs to be there in advance for inspection. They aren't too thorough though. When it gets to Toronto they will inspect them a bit more carefully."

"For drugs or something?" Oren asked.

"Not so much now. They are familiar with my flower business, which is why I always send them to Toronto. Bugs are their major concern."

"Why don't you send them directly to Vancouver?"

"Nothing flies direct to Vancouver and I always avoid any route via the US. I hate dealing with CBP officers."

"So when does your flower shipment have to be at the airport by?"

"At least a day in advance."

"Won't they die?"

Megs laughed. "They'll be in a refrigerated truck."

Oren desperately wanted to call Mother to pass on the shipment information, but it just wasn't an option while he was in the car with Megs and Miguel. He looked at his cell phone and once again he didn't have a signal. He felt that the only way he could get his message through is if he sent a text. The phone would keep trying to re-send it until it finally got through. Oren had a feeling that Mother wouldn't like receiving a text, but at that point he had no choice.

Oren noticed Megs' head was bobbing up and down. She abruptly jolted upright as if she was trying to fight sleep.

"Here Megs. Use my jacket. You're tired, so sleep."

Megs grabbed Oren's coat. "Thanks."

Oren waited a few minutes before he took out his other phone to ensure that Megs was truly sleeping.

Oren quickly texted. "In mountains and no signal. Shipment will be picked up from Gonzalaz's farm this Friday." And put his phone back into his bag.

Although Oren didn't know if the text went through yet, he already started to feel relieved. He stared out the window of the car and took in the beauty of the mountains, the flowers and the cows.

"Watch out!" Oren said.

Miguel swerved out of the way of a cow that walked into the middle of the road, but then lost control of his car and smashed into another cow on the shoulder. The car hit the cow with such force that it veered off the road and slammed into a deep roadside ditch where it came to a rest.

"Oren! Are you okay?" Megs said.

There was no reply.

Megs unbuckled her seatbelt and tried to open up the passenger door. It was jammed, so instead she pulled herself through the opened passenger side window. Once free from the car she opened up the rear door where Oren was; and he was knocked out cold, but he was still breathing. She suspected that he hit his head on the side window, but wasn't 100 percent sure. Megs looked over to Miguel and he was full of blood, but his eyes were opened and he was coherent. It was apparent that his head had slammed into the steering wheel, and it was a miracle that he didn't go through the windscreen since he didn't have his seatbelt on.

Megs first helped Miguel out of the car and he was able to walk on his own. Without any discussion, the two of them helped to pull Oren out of his window and carried him to the side of the road. Within minutes a pickup truck stopped and Oren was placed in the back of the pickup. Megs sat in the back and they drove to the nearest hospital, which was about 40 minutes away.

Megs could hear Oren breathe. His head was cut pretty badly just above the temple, and she gathered that he had a concussion or something. She applied pressure on his cut head to try and stop the bleeding.

"Please be okay. Please be okay." Megs kept saying to herself as tears rolled down her cheeks.

*****

"How is he?" Megs asked the nurse.

"He's responsive. He just got knocked out. Maybe mild concussion," the nurse replied in broken English.

Megs was relieved. After all the commotion Megs didn't even realise until the nurse whisked her away at the hospital that she had a couple of nasty cuts on her face that needed some attention.

Megs was holding Oren's hand when Miguel walked into the hospital room.

Megs walked up to him and gave him a huge hug. "I'm glad you are okay. There's no way you could have avoided those stupid cows."

"Estoy tan triste," Miguel said.

Megs kept trying to reassure Miguel. "It's okay. It's okay."

Miguel let go of Megs and gave her their bags that he recovered from the car.

"Sigue vibrando," Miguel said as he passed Oren's bag to Megs.

168

"It must be his phone. Probably Claire." Megs smiled.

"Muchas gracias Miguel. Now rest!"

Megs sat down on her bed across from Oren and started going through his bag. She took out the other cell phone.

"What the fuck?" she whispered to herself.

She went through his bag and then found his regular cell. Megs was confused.

She saw that there were five missed calls from the other cell phone.

"Who the hell does he know from Colombia?" Megs asked herself.

Megs also noticed that an unread text came through only minutes ago. "When on Friday?"

Megs' heart sunk as she read the previous message.

Megs looked up at Oren, who was still unconscious in a hospital bed, and sympathy quickly turned into hatred.

She needed to stop this from happening. That's when the idea came to her. She grabbed her bags and ran out of the hospital. It didn't take Megs very long before she found a ride with some farmers who were heading to Bogotá.

Chapter 19

Terry was driving in circles. He forgot to ask Claire which block exactly she wanted to meet at, and she wasn't answering her cell phone. A few minutes later he finally spotted her very conspicuous BMW convertible parked in a laneway. Terry parked behind her and got out of the car.

"Where the fuck have you been?"

Terry jumped. "You scared me!"

"Whatever." Claire quickly looked around and opened up the trunk of her car and took out a gas can and spray paint. Terry did the same.

"Did you fill it up?" Claire asked.

"Obviously," Terry replied.

Claire started to walk towards the clinic and Terry followed.

"Wait here. I'm going to open up the back door," Claire said.

A few minutes later Claire appeared. "Pass me a gas can."

Terry did as he was told and Claire went back in and got busy with soaking the entire building.

Claire poked her head out of the door. "Aren't you going to help me?" Terry stood motionless. Claire shook her head and walked over to Terry, grabbing the other gas can and she disappeared into the house again.

Terry kept looking around but the night was silent. By 3 a.m. most people were in a deep sleep. *Perfect time to rob houses.* Terry thought to himself. *Or better yet, set houses on fire.*

Terry's thoughts were interrupted by Claire. He didn't even hear her leave the house. "I need the spray paint."

Claire walked over to the back of the neighbour's shed and wrote with her left hand. "We'll be back." And she then added an anarchy sign as if it was a signature.

Claire walked over to the door and threw the spray paint can into the clinic.

"I'm assuming that you would like me to do the honours?" Claire said.

"No, I'll do it. Just in case there's blowback or something," Terry said.

Claire passed the matches over to Terry. "Get out of here Claire."

But Claire just stepped back to the road.

Terry lit the entire packet of matches on fire and threw it into the house. Both Terry and Claire started running. By the time they reached the car they heard a large booming sound. Their clinic was on fire. Claire's plan had worked.

They both drove off in separate directions.

Claire was initially going directly to her place, but then decided it would be best to talk to Terry about what just happened.

When she reached Terry's house she noticed that he was still in the car. Claire parked her car, walked over to Terry and opened up the passenger door.

"Can we talk?" Claire asked.

Terry didn't say a word, but Claire sat down anyways.

"We had no other option," Claire said.

"I know," Terry said.

"I'm sorry for bringing you in on this, but you are part of the clinic as well and we need to protect ourselves."

Claire rolled down the window and lit a cigarette.

"Do you want one?" Claire asked.

"Normally I would say no, but tonight I need one," Terry replied.

Terry took a long drag and exhaled out of his window.

"I guess we got to get an alibi together. Oren has his being in Colombia and all." Terry took another drag of his cigarette.

"You know he's going to freak out when he finds out we torched the clinic."

"No he won't. It's insured," Claire said.

Terry shrugged his shoulders.

"We were together tonight. I'm going to leave my car at your place."

Claire flicked her cigarette out the window.

"I came over. One drink turned into a couple of bottles of wine and I passed out."

Claire opened up the car door to leave.

"Claire. Stay. You...actually, we shouldn't be alone tonight," Terry said.

Claire smiled. "Sorry Terry. I need to be alone tonight."

Terry grabbed onto Claire's arm. "Please Claire. You can have Ethan's room. It's comfy and painted up with African animals."

Claire smiled and nodded. "Okay."

In actual fact Terry was worried about Claire. He was concerned that she would go home and hit the bottle, cocaine and god knows what else. Although she was strong on the outside, she was quite the emotional person who tried to keep her feelings at bay with narcotics and alcohol. He needed Claire to be completely in control, especially since he assumed that they would have to deal with the police soon.

Terry led Claire up to his apartment and she collapsed on the couch. "Do you want a nightcap?"

"Absolutely," Claire said.

Terry poured a couple of straight whiskeys and brought it over to Claire. "Is this a pullout couch?" Claire asked.

"Yep."

"I'll sleep on this tonight. It's bigger than your kid's toddler bed.

"Ethan's bed is a single anyways. Your feet may dangle off the end, but you are abnormally tall."

Claire gave a friendly punch to Terry's shoulder. "I'm 5 foot, 12. Remember that."

Terry downed his whiskey.

"I don't know how you can do that," Claire said.

"Me neither. I'm tired. Let me pull this out for you. This couch is a bit tricky."

Claire got up and sipped her whiskey as she watched Terry sort out the pull-out couch.

Terry always looked a little bit older than his age, but it was apparent that the divorce or maybe even their illegal clinic was wearing him out. Claire thought that he looked 10 years older than he should as his hair seemed to be receding much more than six months ago, and the crow's feet around his eyes were much more pronounced.

Terry started to make the bed but Claire stopped him. "I'll do the rest Terry. Go to bed."

Terry started to sniff. "Do you smell that Claire? We smell like gasoline."

Claire smelled her jacket, clothes and hands. "It's just my hands. I'll quickly wash up before I go to bed."

"Do you think you'll need a change of clothes?" Terry asked.

"No really Terry. It's just my hands. Now stop worrying about me and go to bed."

Terry nodded and walked straight into his room and collapsed on his bed.

It felt as if only moments went by before he was woken up by the sound of his telephone ringing. And he knew even before answering the phone that it was the police.

Chapter 20

"José! This is Megs. You need to listen carefully."

Megs was in the airport pacing back and forth.

"Oren has deceived me. He is working with a drug cartel and is going to hijack our flower shipment and plant cocaine in Friday's shipment!"

"Dónde estás?" José asked.

"I'm at airport. I want to report it to security."

"Non! Non! Usted nos mataron."

"What?"

"The drug cartels will kill us. All of us," José said.

"Well, what the hell am I supposed to do?" Megs said.

"Get on a flight. Any flight. The soonest flight," José said.

"I can't do that José. I can't just leave."

"You must. I have better idea. You need to get out now. Paris, London, America, anywhere. The soonest flight."

"No. I'm going straight to your farm."

"No! You will kill us. Get out of Colombia. I will sort the rest."

"What's your plan?"

After speaking with José for a few more minutes and then Greta who ensured that the translations was completely understood Megs walked over to the flight departure screen.

Megs then went over to the counter. "One-way ticket to Miami please." And she handed over her passport.

"Have a nice flight Miss. Jiménez Jones." And Megs walked through security.

*****

As José helped his employees load the flower shipment onto the refrigeration truck, he could feel that they were being watched. So he was careful not to do anything out of the ordinary to trigger suspicion or they all would be dead. The thought made him shiver. He looked over to Greta and gave her a smile. Greta started to tear up and walked back into the house.

José informed the driver that he was going to take the shipment to the airport himself and to stay here and look after Greta. The driver argued for a bit, but knew that José was too stubborn to listen to reason.

"Podemos luchar juntos," the driver said.

"Hay combates," José replied.

In the end the driver gave up and watched José hop into the truck and start the engine. Greta walked out of the house and gave José a huge hug and kiss through the driver's side window.

José tried to comfort her. "Será bueno."

Greta let him go and walked back into the house.

José drove off towards the highway to Bogotá International Airport.

He wasn't even on the road for 10 minutes when he noticed two black SUVs appear in his rear view mirror. "Be calm," he told himself. He planned to give them the truck without a fight and hitchhike back to the farm. They would go into hiding until this situation blew over since the drug cartels had other fish to fry. Big fish. Not small fish like him and Greta.

The SUVs accelerated and one passed him stopping just ahead of the truck. The other SUV was right on his tail. It was obvious that they wanted him to stop.

As José waited a man dressed in a black suit and tie got out of the passenger side of the SUV in front of the truck and walked towards José. Once the man reached the driver's side window, without hesitation he pulled out his gun and shot José in the head. He opened the truck door and carried José's lifeless body over to the roadside ditch and rolled him down the hill. The man then walked back to the truck and hopped into the driver's seat. All three vehicles left in convoy.

After about 20 minutes on the highway the convoy peeled off onto a dirt road. Ten minutes later they reached a desolate farm. The SUVs parked in front and the truck drove right into the barn. There were a group of men waiting in the barn. Once parked, the back of the truck was opened and the group of men went into action.

"Slowly slide the capsules into the stems boys. Don't break them," said one of the men who had a lazy eye.

"Jesus, Marco, we're not idiots. If you think you can do better then be my guest," said another man who was sporting a black and white tracksuit.

Marco jumped into the back of the truck and carefully opened up one of the flower boxes.

"Ah shit!" Marco said. "Aphids. Fucking aphids. The flowers are infested with them!"

The men frantically opened the rest of the shipment. "There is no way these will get through customs," Marco said. "Vince. Call the boss."

"Yeah. Sure. Are we in shit?" Vince asked.

"Fuck no. This isn't our fault," Marco said.

Vince explained to the boss what happened with the shipment and in a loud voice that could be heard through the cell phone. "Kill them! Kill them all!"

Vince hung up the phone and looked at Marco.

Marco shrugged his shoulders. "Sounds like Doug is pissed off."

"So who exactly are we supposed to kill?" Vince asked.

Marco whistled to the man in the suit who indiscriminately killed José. It was clear that he was their main assassin.

"Just spoke to the boss. We must kill the doctor, maybe his girlfriend, too." Marco paused. "And torch the farm. Kill whoever we find, but if they had half a brain they'd be gone by now."

The man in the suit nodded and he with two other men hopped into one of the SUV's and drove off.

Chapter 21

Claire turned on her light and picked up her cell. *Why the hell is Megs calling me at midnight on a Monday?* She thought to herself. That was when panic set in as she thought something bad must have happened in Colombia.

"You okay Megs?" Claire asked.

"Yes. No. Can you pick me up at the airport please? I'm alone," Megs said.

"What happened? Where's Oren?"

"He's still in Colombia," Megs started crying.

"Okay. I will be there ASAP. Wait outside in front of arrivals." Claire hung up the phone, quickly got dressed and rushed in her BMW to the airport.

"Why on earth is Megs alone?" Claire said to herself as she drove towards Richmond. Claire was confused, but also very worried. She was especially concerned that Megs left Oren alone in Colombia, a country he has never been before. He couldn't even speak a word of Spanish. *What is Megs thinking?* Claire thought.

When Claire finally got to the airport she spotted Megs right away. She was a mess. She looked tired and anxious.

Claire got out and helped Megs put her bags in the back and gave her a massive hug.

"Please. Let's get out of here," Megs said.

There was silence in the car as Claire drove off. Finally, she couldn't take it anymore.

"What happened Megs? Where's Oren?"

"He's still in Colombia. He deceived me. He's working with the drug cartel." Megs started sobbing.

This made no sense to Claire, but she suspected that Doug had something to do with it.

"What makes you think that?"

"I read his texts and they were going to use my shipment to hide drugs."

"Jesus!"

"Why would he do such a thing to me?"

Claire bit her tongue as she wanted to tell Megs that Doug probably threatened Oren and that he had no choice, but it would have made this whole situation worse; and it would have dragged both her and Terry into it.

"I'm in shock Megs. I just can't believe that Oren would do such a thing. We've been friends for years."

"I know. I was going to marry that bastard."

"Well what's going to happen now?" Claire asked.

"I just want to go home," Megs said.

For the remainder of the drive back to Megs, the two ladies sat in silence. Claire couldn't take it anymore so she turned on the radio.

"I can't help but feel responsible...

I always knew that you were insane...

With your pain...

But I never thought you'd be a junkie because heroin is so passé...

Heroin is so passé...

Heroin is so passé..."

"Turn that shit off!" Megs said.

Claire felt insensitive, but it was an honest mistake. She turned off the radio, but felt the need to defend herself. "It's just the Dandy Warhols. I swear it was totally random. And it's about heroin, not cocaine."

Megs looked out the window and sat in silence.

After what felt like hours, Claire finally made it to Megs and Oren's apartment; and she parked her car in the front of the building.

"I'm going in with you," Claire said.

"You don't have to."

Claire ignored her and entered the building.

Megs turned her key a couple of times and looked up to Claire. "The door is unlocked."

"Maybe you forgot to lock it," Claire said.

Megs shook her head. "I wonder if Oren came home."

Megs opened up her door and the entire apartment was ransacked. Initially Megs was pissed off, but after a quick check she turned white. "Nothing is missing," Megs said.

Megs and Claire backed out of the apartment.

"Let's go to my house and call the cops from there," Claire said.

Both Megs and Claire could feel that something was wrong, so they quickly got back into Claire's BMW.

"Maybe Oren came back in a rage and threw things around", Megs said. She looked over to Claire. "You okay?"

"We're being followed Megs. That fucking SUV was parked outside all this time and it is following us now."

Claire accelerated. "I'll lose the bastard!"

Megs looked back and could see the black SUV tailing them.

Claire was driving like a maniac going through red lights and randomly turning, but she couldn't shake the SUV.

Claire could see that she was coming up to a busy road. It was 10th Avenue and their light was red. Claire accelerated and Megs started screaming. "You're going to kill us Claire!"

Claire ignored Megs and cut right through the red light. Cars were slamming on their brakes, missing the BMW by inches. Fortunately, the SUV wasn't so lucky and was t-boned by a pickup truck.

"Oh my god! Oh my god!" Megs said with her head between her knees.

"Did I lose them?" Claire asked.

Megs looked back. "Yeah. They were hit by a truck."

"Great," Claire said.

"Are we still going to your house?"

"Fuck no. We're going to the Holiday Inn."

"Which one?"

"The one on Howe Street," Claire said. She looked over to Megs and could see that she was shook up.

"I have a cop friend who may still be staying there. He'll be able to help us."

Claire didn't want to rat on Oren, but she could see that this had gotten out of hand.

"If I don't involve the cops, you will die. Maybe even me. We have no other choice."

Megs nodded.

Claire drove her car into the underground parking lot at the Holiday Inn. Claire tried Evan on his cell but there was no answer. Claire planned to keep her car there for a few days, regardless if Evan was there or not, as the drug cartel would be looking for her BMW.

"Could you please tell me which room Evan Mazis is in?" Claire asked the lady at the reception.

Claire couldn't help but think the lady thought they were prostitutes or something since it was just after 1 a.m.

"Is he expecting you?"

"Please tell him that Dr. Claire Lalonde is here to see him. It's a medical emergency."

"Right." The lady said as she rolled her eyes.

After a few rings Evan seemed to have picked up the phone. "Dr. Claire Lalonde is here to see you with another young lady." The receptionist hung up the phone. "He'll be out in a second."

"Thank You," Claire said and waited with Megs on the couch.

About ten minutes went by before Evan made his way out. Right away he could see that something was wrong.

"We need to speak to you. We don't know what to do," Claire said.

"This isn't a good time right now," Evan said.

"It's my entire fault. The drug cartel wants to kill me and I dragged Claire into it," Megs started sobbing.

"Look. Can you please just ask the girl to give us a few minutes of your time and we'll let you get back to what you were doing."

Evan went red. "How did you know? Nevermind... Just give me a few minutes."

Another 10 minutes went by and Megs and Claire looked up to see an attractive brunette in her mid-20s storm out of the hotel.

Evan appeared just behind the girl and he gestured for Megs and Claire to come in.

"I'm in the penthouse," Evan said.

"Good. We can talk in your living room so we don't have to smell sex," Claire said.

"Stop it," Megs whispered to Claire.

"Sorry. I just thought you're trying to patch things up with your wife," Claire said.

Megs butted in. "We're not here to speak with Mr. Mazis about his personal life. We need his help."

"Thank you Miss..." Evan realised that they weren't introduced. "What's your name?"

"I'm Megan Jiménez Jones, but people call me Megs."

"Nice to meet you Megs. Just call me Evan."

Evan led Claire and Megs into his penthouse, and had them take a seat on a couch in the living room.

"Would you like something to drink?"

"Water," Claire said.

"Me too," Megs said.

"Here you go," Evan said and handed them a glass of water each.

"Thanks." Megs and Claire said in unison.

Evan sat on an armchair directly in front of the girls.

"Could you please elaborate with what you said downstairs about the drug cartel?"

"I'm pretty certain that they, as in the drug cartel, were following us in a black SUV from Megs' apartment. I lost them and came directly here," Claire said.

Evan looked uncomfortable. "Did they follow you here?"

"Impossible. They got t-boned at a light," Claire said.

"Let's back up here for a moment. Why do you believe that it was the cartel that was following you? Megs, you said it was your fault."

"I own a flower business and have legit partnerships with farmers all over the world. I try to visit my main farms each year, and this time I decided to bring my fiancé to Colombia with me. I found out while I was there that he made a deal with the drug cartel to smuggle cocaine in my flower shipment. We stopped it, but because of that I think my life is now in danger. And I think I may have dragged Claire into it," Megs' eyes become watery.

"How do you know that your fiancé did this? Are you sure?" Evan asked.

"I read it on his cell phone. They were text messaging back and forth with each other. I read about the deal and then ran away to stop it."

"Who is your fiancé?"

Megs hesitated. "What will happen to him?"

"He'll probably go to jail assuming he's still alive," Evan said.

Megs broke down and started to cry.

Claire leaned over and hugged Megs. "Jesus, Evan. Can you be a little more sympathetic?"

"I'm sorry; I'm not trying to be an asshole." Evan took a deep breath and continued. "But I need his name. I'll try my best to locate him as it is in my best interest, too."

"Oren O'Brian," Megs said.

Evan was surprised. "Your fiancé is Oren O'Brian?"

Megs nodded. "Do you know him or something?"

"We've been questioning him about his holistic clinic."

Claire felt like she was going to die.

"What holistic clinic?" Megs was shocked.

Claire jumped in and looked at Megs. "I'm in on it with Oren. We started a holistic clinic to get some extra money."

"What..." Megs was interrupted by Claire. "We knew that you would see through us because we don't believe in homeopathy. We deceived our patients in thinking we did. I'm sorry Megs."

"Who else is in on it?" Megs asked.

"Terry. And he needed the money the most. He owed so much money to the lawyers. You know how dirty his divorce was."

Megs got up off of the couch and stared intensely at Claire. "You guys are such assholes!"

Claire looked down and tried her best to look ashamed. "I know."

"Can't you arrest her for lying to patients?" Megs said.

"There's nothing illegal about selling homeopathic remedies. I can't see it being any different than those silly psychics. But it does raise a more serious question." Evan looked at Claire. "If Oren is truly working for the drug cartel, he may have used the holistic clinic to do much of his dealings. And it could also have something to do with why your clinic was burned down."

"The clinic was burned down?" Megs asked.

"By the Anti-Gentrification Front," Claire said.

"Allegedly," Evan said and stood up. "Before you say anything else I am going to take both of you down to the station."

"Are you arresting us?" Claire asked.

"For what? I need to get you two into protective custody right away. I have a feeling you two are in deeper shit than you realise."

Claire was actually relieved with this. There was no way she wanted to venture back to her apartment alone. Then it dawned on her. "What about Terry Wu?"

"I'll send a cruiser over to his house to keep an eye on it," Evan said.

"He has a son," Claire said.

"Don't worry Claire. We got it covered," Evan said.

Evan grabbed his coat. "I'll go downstairs to the parking lot first and make sure it's clear. Once I do, I will phone my hotel room, and I want you guys to use the back stairwell as well as the back entrance into the underground parking lot. I'm lot 23."

Claire and Megs nodded.

"My car is parked down there too," Claire said.

"Good. And that's where it is going to stay for the time being," Evan said.

Evan left closing the door quietly behind him.

It took Evan over 15 minutes to call them and for that whole time Megs didn't even look at Claire.

Neither of the girls spoke to each other for the entire drive to the station. Claire could tell that Megs was extremely upset and wished she'd be her usual confrontational self.

Chapter 22

It has been two weeks since Megs was placed in protective custody. Claire's life wasn't considered to be in danger as much as Megs, but that was because the police didn't know how involved she was in Doug's drug business. They told her that out of precaution they would have the police monitor her apartment as well as Terry's. Claire knew that the real interest was with Oren, and that they thought he may eventually show up at either of his colleague's houses. They probably were even monitoring his father's house.

"You are here again Dr. Lalonde," a police officer said.

"Yes. I need to speak with my best friend," Claire said. She showed up every day for the past two weeks and attempted to reconnect with Megs, who did not want to speak with her.

The police officer knocked on Megs' hotel room door. "Dr. Lalonde is here and she wants to speak with you."

"Tell her to go away," Megs shouted through the door.

"Give me two minutes Megs. If you don't like what I have to say then I will leave you alone. If not, I will come here and bug you every single day."

Megs stayed quiet behind the door.

"Two minutes Megs. That's all I ask. I promise I will leave you alone after that, but please give me those two lousy minutes."

Megs opened up the door and looked at Claire straight in her face. "Two minutes. That's it."

Claire walked into the hotel room closing the door behind them.

"How are you?" Claire asked.

"Fantastic. I can't work and I'm stuck here all the time as they need to protect their key witness. I'm a witness against not only my fiancé, but bad-ass drug cartels, too. All because of you and Oren."

Claire looked directly at Megs. "I had nothing to do with it. I had no idea that Oren was working with the drug cartel. I swear, Megs."

"I don't believe you."

"I have been interrogated by the cops for hours about it. And they let me go because even they believed me. I had nothing to do with this Megs."

"My warehouse has been closed and is part of the investigation now. My employees have no clue why they can't work. I somehow managed to lose my cell phone, and I haven't even been allowed to go to my warehouse and collect my address book. I can't even call my famers and tell them why I haven't been ordering from them for that past two weeks. I worked so hard to get this business going and you and Oren ruined it. You guys are such selfish assholes."

"I had nothing to do with this Megs."

"If you had never started that clinic with him then this would have never happened. And I'm sure the clinic was your idea."

"Actually, it was Oren's. I went along with it and for that I take responsibility. But what other illegal activities he was involved with I was not part of it."

"Yeah right," Megs said.

Claire was getting frustrated. "And I think you're a hypocrite."

"What the hell does that supposed to mean?"

"The selling of illicit drugs helped you through university. It paid your way. And now you are being all self-righteous about it."

"That's so fucking different, Claire. I grew my own weed and sold it myself. My weed didn't cause war, death and destruction like cocaine does."

Megs walked towards Claire. "Because of cocaine one of my farmers lost both of his kids. Families have been destroyed. For what? Our little 15 minutes of feeling good because us in Western society feels so goddamn sorry for ourselves. We are completely oblivious to what kind of damage it has done to countries like Colombia and Mexico."

Megs opened up the door. "Get the hell out of here or I'll ask the police to remove you."

Claire swallowed her pride and walked out. She had enough of Megs, and she knew there was no way of getting through to her.

*****

Claire sat in her car in the hotel parking lot and started to cry. She cried for nearly 10 minutes bashing her hands on the steering wheel. Not only was she frustrated and angry at Megs, but she was also worried about Oren. After talking to Megs reality set it. Either the police or the drug cartel was going to take him down. And that was assuming that he was still alive. Last week Evan gave Claire the heads up that Oren may be in touch with her. Apparently he landed in Toronto, and they suspected that he was travelling by land back to Vancouver. She wasn't sure how long the police knew of this, but didn't care as she was relieved that he wasn't killed in Colombia. She hoped that Oren knew what danger he was in and would go straight to the police. She desperately wanted to get a hold of him, but his cell phone was going straight to voice mail. It was evident that he either shut it off or it was lost.

Claire looked at the time. She had to get to the clinic for her shift in 15 minutes. "Get yourself together," Claire said to herself.

After a few more minutes in the car calming herself down, Claire drove to work.

*****

Claire was having a hard time concentrating at the clinic. She needed something to help calm her nerves. She peered over to the cabinet in the hallway. It was filled with pain relievers such as ibuprofen and not so innocent opioid-based narcotics. When the hallway was clear Claire ran over to the cabinet and grabbed a pack of morphine pills. She casually walked back to her office and closed the door.

Claire swallowed two pills and closed her eyes. She kept visualizing Oren's body in a ditch full of flies and maggots. She opened them straight away. That image would pop into her head all of the time. It even haunted her in her dreams.

Claire looked at the time. She wasn't even half done her shift, so she got up and left her office.

"Who's next?" Claire asked one of the resident doctors.

"Room two. He's complaining about a shoulder problem."

Claire grabbed the file and walked into the room. She closed the door and smiled at a man with dark hair in his mid to late 40s. He was wearing a track suit.

"How can I help you?" Claire asked.

"A few days ago I fell off of a ladder and my left shoulder is getting worse by the day. Hurts like a bitch, but I don't think it's dislocated."

"It may be separated. Can I take a look?"

The man nodded.

Claire walked over to him and started analysing his shoulder and arm.

The man then put a knife to Claire's throat and covered her mouth.

"You better not scream or I'll slit your throat. I just need you to answer a question."

Claire nodded yes.

"Where's Oren O'Brian?" The man slowly removed his hand from Claire's mouth, but kept the blade firmly up against her neck.

"I don't know."

The man pushed the blade even further into her neck.

"I swear I don't know. I've been consistently calling his cell phone, but it goes directly to voice mail."

"You have to do better than that," the man said.

"I don't know where he is. I'm looking for him, too. Check my phone. I've tried calling him thousands of times."

"Do you have your phone with you?"

"Yes. It's in my pocket."

"Which pocket?"

"Bottom left in my lab coat."

The man reached into Claire's pocket and removed the cell phone.

He scrolled through the history and selected Oren's phone number and put it up against Claire's ear.

"It's his voice mail. See for yourself," Claire said.

The man listened to the voice mail on Claire's phone.

"We're watching you. Don't think those stupid cops watching over your house will stop us either. If we find out you're lying to us, you're dead."

Claire nodded and the man relaxed his arm and put the knife in his pocket.

"And if you tell your cop friends about today, I'll personally kill you. I haven't gotten laid in a while."

The man got up and left the patient room, and Claire just sat in there stunned. She wasn't sure what would be more horrifying: that asshole raping her or dying. She shuddered at the thought.

Claire reached down into her pocket and took another morphine pill. She needed as much help as she could get to get through the rest of the day.

*****

After working for a few more hours at the walk-in-clinic, Claire couldn't take it anymore. Even the narcotics weren't calming her down enough to focus on her patients. She needed to talk to Terry.

Claire went into her office and shut the door. She tried calling Terry's cell phone, but he didn't answer it. So she then tried phoning his home phone and yet again there was no answer. Claire started to wonder if he also got a warning from one of Doug's men. *Most probably.* She thought to herself.

Claire didn't want to risk going to Terry's house because she was certain his house was also being watched. "Could he be at work?" Claire asked herself.

She started sifting through her cell phone and brought up a schedule from a few months ago when they were still working at the pseudo-holistic clinic. Claire would have had a shift today, which would normally mean that Terry would be working at his real medical clinic. With this new revelation Claire quickly phoned the clinic.

"Hi. This is Dr. Lalonde and I'm looking for a Dr. Terry Wu."

"I'm sorry he's not here," the receptionist replied.

"He's supposed to be working today. Is he sick?" Claire asked.

The receptionist hesitated for a few seconds and then finally replied. "He never showed up for his shift today."

"Well that's very strange," Claire said.

"Yes. It's out of character. Anything else, doctor?"

"No. Thank you." And Claire slowly hung up the phone.

Claire was certain that Doug had him killed.

"Fuck," Claire said out loud and she started to pace back and forth in her office.

Regardless what the risks were, Claire needed to go to Terry's house.

She took off her lab coat and grabbed her purse. On her way out of the clinic she told the receptionist that there was a family emergency. Claire was gone before the receptionist had time to respond.

Claire hopped in her car and drove to Terry's. She parked a few blocks away and carefully walked to his apartment. Straight away she could see that his car wasn't there. She walked back to her car and drove to his old house where his ex-wife and Ethan lived. His car wasn't there either.

Claire didn't know what to do so she started to drive around areas of Vancouver that she knew Terry frequented, including local parks.

Claire was no longer thinking rationally and decided to go home. But then she remembered the warning she received earlier that day. The thought of her house being watched made her feel uneasy. She started panicking and pulled over to the side of the road. Claire put her car in park and started banging the steering wheel. She didn't know where to go or what to do, and she couldn't shake the thought of Terry's potential death out of her head.

"Fuck, fuck, fuck!" Claire screamed over and over again. She then jumped at the sound of her cell phone. A text just came in.

She grabbed her phone and relief set in immediately.

"Meet me at Falconetti's. I'm there now." It was Terry.

Once Claire was back on the road she started to wonder if it was indeed Terry. She quickly shook the thought out of her head. She didn't think Doug would have known about their usual watering hole.

Claire parked her car quite a few blocks away from Falconetti's. She assumed that the drug cartel may know what her car looks like so she wanted to keep it off of the main roads.

She put a hat on, as well as sunglasses, and quickly walked to the bar.

When she entered the bar she had to walk around Falconetti's a couple of times before finding Terry. He was in a dark corner staring at his half empty pint.

Claire walked over and sat down in front of him.

Terry looked up. "Hey."

"Hey yourself. What's going on? I've been looking for you all day. I thought you were..." Claire couldn't finish her sentence.

"Did they find you?"

"This morning one of my patients stuck a blade to my throat. He said that if I lied to him about Oren's whereabouts then he'll personally kill me. Actually, he insinuated that he'd rape me first and then kill me." Claire's voice became quite shaky.

"Jesus, Claire." Terry grabbed her hand. "How did you get out of it?"

"I told him that I have also been trying to get a hold of Oren. He saw my cell phone, including my history of how many times I've called Oren. That asshole also called Oren on my phone and it went directly to his voice mail. It was enough evidence I guess."

"I also got a visit early this morning. I was about to leave for work and there was a guy in a black balaclava hiding in the back seat of my car. He also put a knife up to my throat. He then asked me where Oren was. After telling him a bunch of times that I didn't know as he pushed the blade further into my neck, he finally let go. He also told me that if I lied to him that my kid would die." Terry's voice started to shake.

"Fuck Claire. They know Ethan's name, his school, where he lives, everything!"

Terry took a deep breath and carried on. "Do you know why they are keeping us alive?"

Claire shook her head as she sincerely didn't know.

"We're bait. They want Oren and as soon as he shows up on one of our doorsteps, we're all dead."

A waitress came over and put a glass of water in front of Claire.

"Would you like to order a drink?"

"Just a glass of your house red."

Terry and Claire didn't say a word to each other while they waited for the waitress to come back with the glass of wine.

When the waitress finally returned Claire took a couple of sips and put the glass down. "I don't feel like drinking."

"My pint isn't going down very well either," Terry said.

"I don't understand why they want to kill us Terry. We weren't involved with that shit in Colombia."

"First of all, they don't know how much we know about that."

Claire interrupted. "But we don't know anything!"

"We're disposable Claire. If Oren shows up at my place, they won't hesitate to come in and put a bullet through my head, too. They can't risk anything."

Claire bit her lip. She felt defeated.

Terry downed the rest of his beer. "I'm staying at a hotel tonight. I suggest you do the same thing."

"You know the cops are also watching our apartments."

"Well, if Oren shows up at my place, I won't be in. I'm not risking it."

Terry took a $10 bill out of his wallet and put it on the table. "I'll see you around. Stay safe and good luck."

When he stood up he gently squeezed Claire's shoulder and walked out of the bar. Claire had a feeling that would be the last time she would see Terry in a while.

Claire left another $10 bill on the table and went to the washroom. She phoned Evan. "Hey. It's me, Claire."

"Hey. You okay? You sound upset."

"I'm just a little spooked about this whole thing. Are you guys still watching my place?"

"Yeah. Don't worry Claire. We have someone watching you around the clock."

"Okay. Thanks."

"You're safe Claire. I won't let anything happen to you."

"Thanks Evan. I guess I just needed a bit of reassurance."

"Well, I got to get back to work. You take care of yourself Claire."

Claire said good-bye and hung up the phone.

She closed her eyes and started crying. The harder she tried to compose herself the more she cried.

After a few minutes Claire got herself together and with confidence she walked out of the washroom, out of Falconetti's and into the street. She wasn't going to let Doug control her life.

Chapter 23

Just like clockwork at 8 a.m. everyday there was a knock on Megs' hotel room door. She answered it and, as usual, it was room service bringing her breakfast.

Megs smiled at the hotel employee as he wheeled her meal in and placed it on the table in front of the television.

"Thank you," Megs said and she sat down and opened the silver lid covering her breakfast. There staring back at her was scrambled eggs, two pieces of bacon, two slices of whole wheat toast, a mug of coffee and a glass of grapefruit juice. Megs was tired of the same old breakfast, and she desperately wanted a room with a kitchenette so that she could cook for herself.

Megs took a couple of bites of her bacon and slammed it down on her plate. "This is so shitty." She said out loud.

Megs walked over to the hotel room door and opened it up.

"Can we talk?" Megs asked the police officer who was guarding her door.

"Sure."

"I need someone to take me to my warehouse. I have business that I must finish."

"As we told you a hundred times before, it's too risky."

"Can I speak with your supervisor then?"

"Not this again. You know that I've spoken to her. She even came down here and explained it to you herself how dangerous it is to let you leave."

"It's been over two weeks. How long are you going to keep me cooped up in the god- forsaken hotel room?"

"Like we've told you many times before, we need to find your fiancé."

Megs interrupted. "He's not my fiancé."

196

"We need to find Oren O'Brian and we believe that we're close. We need our key witness kept alive."

"Can I at least change rooms? Can I get one with a kitchenette? I'm going to lose my mind here."

"I don't see why not, but I need to call my supervisor first. It may be safer having you move rooms, too."

"Thank you," Megs said and she shut the door.

Megs walked back over to the couch and looked at her breakfast. She had no appetite, but managed to drink her coffee and grapefruit juice while watching Canada AM.

After a few minutes she changed the channel. It was yet another morning show. Not even two minutes went by before a commercial came on. She changed the channel again.

"Shit. TV is full of shit," Megs said out loud. She turned the television off and threw the remote control beside her on the couch.

Megs got up and grabbed her book that was laying on her bed. Whatever she wanted the police would pick it up for her. So far on behalf of the taxpayers, she had seven new books to add to her collection. Megs longed for her library. At home she had a couple of bookshelves filled with novels. Then she shuddered. "Our home." Megs started to cry but sadness quickly turned into anger. Once again she questioned how Oren could deceive her and how many more lies he had told. She didn't want to live in the same house, but she wanted her stuff. And she wanted to burn anything that would remind her of Oren.

Megs then started to wonder where he was. Jeff, who seemed to spend the most amount of time guarding her, said that the police were close; but he wouldn't give her anymore details than that. And Megs knew that finding Oren was only the beginning. The police weren't afraid of Oren hurting Megs, they were afraid of the drug cartel killing them both. From overhearing a few conversations, there are some

197

dangerous people working for the drug cartel that the police have been chasing for years. One man named Douglas van der Merwe was brought up numerous times. The police tried to nail him so many times in the past, but couldn't really pin anything on him. And to Megs' dismay, they believed that Oren was working for him. Meg assumed that Oren would be given a plea bargain if he gave evidence to pin down this van der Merwe guy.

This would be an exciting story if I wasn't involved. Megs thought to herself.

Megs' thoughts were interrupted by a knock on her door.

Megs opened the door and smiled at Jeff. He was actually quite cute and carried the shaved head look really well. He was a bit too young for her, but he had a big heart and other than allow her to leave the hotel room, he would ensure that she got what she wanted.

"So I called the boss and she says moving you is a great idea."

Megs smiled.

"It gets better. We got you a kitchenette; and if you stop asking to leave the hotel every day, I will promise to buy you whatever groceries you need so that you can cook for yourself."

"Jeff, you're awesome," Megs said.

"Do you want to pack up? The room is available now."

"Perfect."

Megs ran over to the bed and started packing her things.

Another police officer came to the door to help Megs' move to the other room. Alex was another young police officer who was posted to watch her room. He always seemed really bored and she couldn't blame him. Going through extensive police training to stand in front of a door for hours on end had to be tough. Megs pitied all of her police guards.

"Are you ready?" He grabbed her bags and both Jeff and Alex escorted Megs through the corridor and into the elevator. Jeff pushed the button for the second floor.

For such a nice hotel the elevator seemed so old and loud. It came to a halt with such abrasive force that Megs had to steady herself.

When the doors opened the three of them walked down the hall and turned into the next corridor. It looked like Megs had a corner room.

Jeff opened up the door. "Here you go Madam."

Megs walked in and the room must have been double the size of her previous one. And, as promised, there was a kitchenette.

"This is perfect. Thanks so much guys."

"No problem Megs, but remember our deal," Jeff said.

Megs smiled and nodded.

"So do you want to write a grocery list out? I'm sure you're dying to do your own cooking."

"Oh my god, yes!" she replied.

Right away Megs grabbed a hotel pad and pen and started scribbling down her list.

"This is a good start," Megs said and handed the paper over to Jeff.

"Nice list. Can you share whatever you're making with me? I'm sick and tired of Burger King and McDonald's."

"Of course," Megs said.

Jeff and Alex smiled at Megs and closed the door.

As soon as the door clicked shut, Megs locked the door as she was instructed to do. She then walked over to the window and peered out.

"I can totally jump two floors," Megs said as she looked down.

Megs gazed across the road and noticed an undercover police car. They were patrolling around the hotel, so if she were going to make a quick escape her timing would have to be perfect.

*****

Megs was nearly finished cooking paella con carne. Jeff couldn't find Arborio rice so he bought plain white rice instead. It wasn't the first time Megs was stuck with the wrong rice. She remembered when she asked Oren to pick up some groceries for her, including Arborio rice, and he claimed he couldn't find it. It was one of the first meals she cooked for Oren, who had such bland taste in food. He was so sceptical about paella, but absolutely loved it in the end. It was one of his favourite meals that Megs would cook for him. Megs started to tear up, but she quickly pushed that thought away.

Megs served up the paella in a couple of dishes and opened up the hotel room door. "Pour vous."

"Thanks Megs. It smells so damn good. I haven't had this since I visited Spain in my high school years."

Megs kept the door opened and dragged a chair over. "Can we at least eat together?"

"Yeah, of course," Jeff said.

"When are you done your shift?" Megs asked. "You've been here all day."

"I'm staying on just for a couple more hours. Do you remember Constable Don Edwards?"

"Is he the pudgy officer with glasses?"

Jeff laughed. "Yeah. That's him. He's going to be a few hours late, which is fine by me. Otherwise, I would have missed this meal."

Megs only spoke to Constable Edwards a few times before. He would normally do the nightshift, and only a couple times per week, so Megs wouldn't see him that much.

"Do you want some more?" Megs asked.

"No, this is perfect. Your paella is amazing. Just how I remembered it."

"Even with the wrong rice?"

"Sorry about that. But I blame Alex. He should have picked up your groceries instead of me. He's more of a food connoisseur."

"I don't think he would have done that for me."

"Of course he would have. You're one of his favourites. And he wants you to save him some paella for tomorrow."

"Well, I made enough for a few days."

"Perfect."

Megs took Jeff's plate to wash up and they said their good-byes.

"I'll see you in a few days. I have tomorrow off," Jeff said.

"Sounds good," Megs said and she closed the door.

While Megs was cleaning up the kitchen she could hear Constable Edwards' voice. He must have finally arrived to take over from Jeff.

Megs sat down on the couch and started reading. Occasionally she would look out the window to try and spot the undercover police car.

When Megs peered out the window for about the 20th time in the hour she saw the police car drive away. He would occasionally move to another spot around the hotel's perimeter. Megs gathered that he moved to the front of the hotel to keep an eye on who was coming and going from the hotel.

Megs quietly opened the window. Another quick look around and she saw and heard nobody, so she took that chance and jumped out onto the ground.

She initially kept close to the hotel's outer walls and peered around the corner of the building. It was clear. She looked up and down the road. There was no one in sight, so she casually walked across the street and headed north. Megs flagged down the first taxi she saw and hopped in. She gave the driver the address to her flower warehouse. She was hoping that by the time she made a few phone calls to her main clients and cabbed it back to the hotel, sneaking in again, no one would even notice. Megs thought about José and Greta. Those would be the first people she'd call. She needed to see that they were alright.

"Thanks. Keep the change," Megs said to the driver after reaching the warehouse.

Once the taxi drove away Megs felt alone in the parking lot; so she quickly entered the warehouse, locking the door behind her. Claire noticed that the office lights were on so she walked directly towards it. Her office was empty so she assumed that the lights were left on by accident. She sat down and opened up the desk drawer, grabbing her address book.

Megs found José's number and tried calling it. There was no answer so Megs hung up.

Megs was so busy thumbing through her address book that she didn't notice a dark shadow appear at the door way.

"Hello my darling," Oren said.

Megs' heart jumped and she quickly stood up. "What are you doing here?"

"Hiding, I assumed that this is one of the only places that Doug and his goons don't know about. And since they want to kill me all thanks to you, I thought staying here would be my best chance of survival."

"You deceived me. You ruined by business."

Oren took a few steps into the office and Megs could see him clearly in the light. He was haggard with dark rings around his eyes, and he looked about 10 years older. But what Megs couldn't shake was the hate she saw in his eyes; and she knew it was directed at her.

"This wasn't my fault. You used me," Megs said.

"Ever since I woke up from my accident I have been on the run. First, I find out that you ran off, leaving me to rot in the hospital. I then get a call from an unidentified man who tells me that I'm dead. After putting two and two together, I realise that you've gone to tell the cops. In my shitty condition I managed to pay a couple of farmers to hide me in the back of their pickup and take me directly to the airport. I couldn't find you anywhere and assumed that you were long gone."

"None of that was my fault. You were going to use my flower shipment to smuggle drugs into Canada. I can't believe you would do such a thing."

Oren took a few steps closer towards Megs. "I eventually ended up in Toronto because I thought it would be a safer route. I spent over a week hitchhiking back to Vancouver. And I'm so happy that I trusted my intuition because when I had a peak at our apartment, I noticed a couple of suspicious-looking black SUVs parked outside. And I wasn't sure if they were undercover cops or Doug's men ready to kill me."

"You aren't the only one that they are trying to kill, Oren. You dragged me in this shit with you."

Megs backed into the wall. She was cornered and Oren was walking towards her. He was close enough that she could see into the depths of his eyes. His pupils were dilated.

"You're fucked up on drugs," Megs said.

Oren stopped. "Just a little bit of coke to make the pain go away. Do you know how many truckers use it as a little pick-me-up?"

Megs' heart sank as she realised that Oren was volatile. She had no clue how long he was on his coke-fuelled binge for and he was clearly acting crazy. Rationalizing with him was not an option in his state.

Megs looked around the room and eyed the baseball bat in the corner of her office. That thing was in the corner of the room collecting dust for years. She gathered it was left there by one of her employees, and Megs was about to put it to good use.

She grabbed the baseball bat and held it up in the air. "Back the fuck up!"

Oren started laughing. "Are you actually going to hit me, my dear?"

Megs took a swing and missed. Oren started laughing. "Kitty got claws!"

Oren went towards her and wrestled the bat from her hands, pushing her onto the ground.

Without hesitation he slammed the baseball bat onto the side of her head, knocking her out. "How do you like it?"

Megs didn't move.

"Answer me!"

Oren started to shake her. "Wake up!"

Oren dropped the bat and started crying.

"Please wake up. I didn't mean it. Please, please wake up."

Oren stood up and walked out of the office. He started slamming his hands against the warehouse walls and screaming.

Oren walked towards the back of the warehouse where the loading bay was located. He opened the back door and noticed Megs' delivery trucks.

Oren went back into the office, and the sight of Megs' lifeless body crumpled in the corner of the room triggered him to cry again.

He grabbed a set of keys on the hook next to the desk and walked back to the trucks. Oren tried to open the doors of the various delivery trucks until he found the correct one. He then hopped into the driver's seat and put the keys in the ignition, starting the truck. He put the truck into reverse and looked at himself in the rear view mirror.

After a few minutes of just staring at his reflection, Oren put the truck into park and hopped out, leaving the truck in idle.

Oren grabbed a hose pipe from the warehouse and attached it on the inside of the exhaust pipe. He cracked opened the passenger side window and slid the other side of hose pipe into the window.

Oren jumped back into the truck carefully closing the door.

He turned on the radio and changed the channel until he found Fox FM. He then laid back and closed his eyes, listening to the DJs babble on about nothing.

Oren let all the pain go and eventually fell asleep.

Chapter 24

Claire was nearly done her afternoon shift at the clinic. She went into the office, locked the door, and collapsed on the chair. She saw her cell phone flashing on the desk and picked it up. She had seven missed calls from Evan. Claire instantly thought that they had found Oren. Her heart started to beat quickly. "Please be alive," Claire said to herself as she dialed Evan's number.

Claire barely heard the first ring before Evan picked it up. "Claire."

Claire hesitated. "Hi Evan."

"A lot of shit has gone down in the last 24 hours. I need to see you at Vancouver General immediately."

"I refuse to go unless you tell me what's going on."

"Megs is in the hospital, but she will be okay. She has a concussion. Oren slammed a baseball bat on the side of her head. I think she is more psychologically damaged than anything else."

"It couldn't have been Oren."

"I hate to say it, but it was."

Claire interrupted Evan. "Is Oren in jail then?"

"I'd rather tell you in person Claire."

"He's not in jail is he? He's dead. Tell me what happened."

Evan took a deep breath. "He killed himself Claire. We suspect that it was carbon monoxide poisoning."

Claire started crying and Evan waited patiently.

"This is so fucking crazy," Claire said.

"I know," Evan said.

After Claire stopped crying Evan continued.

"I need you at the hospital now Claire. A police car is already on its way to pick you up."

"Will Megs even see me?"

"You have to be strong, Claire. We need someone to identify Oren's body."

"No way!"

"Claire, listen to me. Megs is in no state to do it, and Oren's father is in complete denial that his son is dead. You were Oren's colleague and I suspect that you two were very close."

Claire remained silent. After a few minutes Evan spoke up. "Are you still there?"

"I'll do it." Claire hung up the phone.

Claire opened up her purse and found some Valium. She popped a couple of pills in her mouth, grabbed her jacket and walked out of the office.

"Are you alright Dr. Lalonde?" asked one of the nurses.

"No. One of my friends is in the hospital and I have to identify the body of another."

Before the nurse had anytime to respond, Claire was walking out the clinic door. A police car was already waiting out front.

Claire sat quietly in the back of the police car staring out the window as they headed to the hospital. She dreaded the moment when she would see Oren's body. She regretted agreeing to it, but then again it was not like she had a choice.

I hope we get in a goddamn car accident. Claire thought to herself as she desperately wanted to put a stop to this long and horrendous drive to the hospital.

The police car finally pulled up in front of the hospital and Claire saw Evan straight away. He was on his cell phone pacing back and forth in front of the automatic doors. Claire didn't think he realised that every time he would pace in front of the doors they would automatically open. *Those in the foyer must be getting annoyed.* Claire thought to herself.

When Evan saw Claire get out of the car, he quickly got off the phone and walked over to Claire and gave her a hug.

"I'm so sorry Claire," Evan said.

Claire fought hard to keep her tears back. "I just want to get this over and done with."

"Follow me," Evan said as he escorted her to the elevator and they went to the basement floor.

"Why are morgues always in the basement?" Claire said.

Evan was surprised. "You've never been down here before?"

"Of course I have, but this time it's different."

Claire followed Evan into the office, and there was a lady with short black hair sitting at the desk going through paperwork. She looked up and smiled at Evan. "So this is the lady who will be identifying the body?"

"Yes," Evan said.

Claire didn't recognise the technician, so she leaned over the desk and shook her hand.

"I'm Dr. Claire Lalonde. It's been a while since I've worked at Vancouver General. Did you just start working here?"

"I'm Connie Tung. I just moved to Vancouver from Victoria a few months ago."

"Nice to meet you," Claire said.

"Are you ready?" Connie asked.

Claire nodded.

Connie led Oren and Claire into one of the far rooms. After locating Oren's body she looked up at Claire. "I'm going to move the sheets back so that you can see his face."

Claire took a deep breath. "Okay."

Connie removed the sheet and looked at Claire.

Claire closed her eyes and re-opened them after a few seconds. Oren looked as if he was sleeping peacefully. His rosy cheeks were a telltale sign that he died of carbon monoxide poisoning.

"Is this Oren O'Brian?" Evan asked.

"Yes. It's him." Claire's voice started to break.

Connie quickly put the sheet back over his face and Evan escorted her out of the room.

"Thanks Connie," Evan said as he quickly got Claire out of the morgue.

"I know that was hard Claire and I can't thank you enough for being so strong. We can now continue with our investigation and figure out what the hell happened."

"Does Megs know?" Claire asked.

"Yeah, I told her. Thought she'd feel safer knowing that he was dead, but it made her more distraught."

Claire wanted to call Evan an idiot, but she bit her tongue.

"Megs is on the fourth floor. Room 412, I believe."

"Thanks," Claire said as she made her way over to the elevator.

"I'll be in touch soon," Evan said.

Claire knew that she was going to be interrogated because of her connection with Oren. She would have to choose her words very carefully so as not to slip up on what was really happening in their so-called holistic clinic. The clinic that started out as such a good idea turned into a nightmare as soon as Doug forced his way in. And Oren ultimately paid with his life.

When Claire reached Megs' hospital room she looked in the window. Megs was sitting up watching TV with her mother.

Claire knocked on the door and peeked in.

Megs looked up and before she had a chance to say anything, Claire ran over and gave Megs a hug. Claire started crying and then Megs followed suit.

"I saw him. His father wouldn't see him so I had to," Claire said and she squeezed Megs tighter. "What the hell happened?"

Megs gently pushed Claire back, and held her at shoulder length, looking into her eyes. "It wasn't Oren. He was messed up on drugs and didn't sleep for days. Our Oren would have never done that."

Claire nodded. "I guess that's why he couldn't live with himself. When he saw what he did to you."

Megs just shrugged her shoulders.

Claire completely forgot that Megs' mother was in the room. She came over with a box of Kleenex.

"Thanks Maria," Claire said.

"I have to get going anyways. I'll let you two girls talk," Maria said.

She gave Megs a big hug. "When are you going to be discharged from this dreadful place?"

"Either this evening or tomorrow sometime."

"Okay, let me know because I'm picking you up and taking you home."

Claire knew she wasn't talking about Megs and Oren's apartment. Claire didn't know how Megs would cope with disposing of Oren's stuff.

"I want to burn that apartment down." It was as if Megs was reading Claire's thoughts.

"I can help you," Claire said.

"Burn it down?" Megs asked.

"No. Get rid of his stuff. Or pack. I'm assuming you're not going to stay there."

"God no, I wonder if the drug cartels will still be after me?" Megs said.

"I don't know. Either way, Evan will send some police officers there. You'll be protected."

Megs looked at Claire with stern eyes. "I'm not going to live in fear."

Claire nodded in agreement. "Of course not."

After a few minutes of silence Megs spoke up. "What about his funeral? I don't know if I can organise it. Do you think his father will?"

"His father is a nut job. He doesn't even believe that his son is dead." Claire took a deep breath. "Don't worry, I'll organise it Megs."

"Thanks," Megs said.

"I think the first thing I'll have to do is convince Mr. O'Brian that his son died." Claire closed her eyes and tried desperately to stop herself from crying again. "This is just a head fuck."

Megs hugged Claire again. "We both have to be strong."

Chapter 25

Like most funerals that were a result of a tragedy, it was very sombre. Oren's colleagues, friends and family didn't crack a joke or even talk about the good old times. Barely anyone spoke. The rumour that was going around was that Oren was involved with a drug cartel and had become a druggie. He then beat up Megs and killed himself. Claire desperately wanted to tell people the truth, that Oren had no choice to work with the drug cartel; but it would expose both her and Terry. She couldn't risk it. She tried to rationalise it by telling herself that it was for the safety and well-being of Terry's son Ethan, but Claire also didn't want to go down for their mistake. She only wanted to close this chapter of her life and start from new.

Even though Oren wasn't religious and didn't even believe in God for that matter, the vicar at the Anglican Church agreed to lead the memorial service. The vicar did a great job keeping his service as humanistic as possible. Now and then he would talk about God and heaven, but it wasn't for Oren. Claire didn't actually believe that memorial services were for the dead, but rather for those who were left grieving. So she was hoping this mix would appease those who were believers and those who were not. Megs' mother, in particular, was a practising Catholic who loved Oren before he decided to attack her daughter. And Claire thought that Maria needed to hear that God mumbo jumbo to make her feel more comfortable at her would be son-in-law's funeral.

Claire began to fight her tears. Terry was sitting beside her and grabbed her hand.

Claire whispered in his ear. "If it wasn't for that clinic we would be having a wedding, not a goddamn funeral."

Terry closed his eyes and nodded. Terry was actually relieved that Oren was dead. He felt certain that his son was safe now since Doug ultimately got what he wanted.

Claire was about to say something else to Terry, but the vicar called out her name. Claire was the only person who agreed to speak at Oren's funeral.

Claire let go of Terry's hand and she walked up to the front of the church.

Claire looked around and she saw Megs, who was sitting beside her mother and aunt who flew in from Toronto. She, too, was very fond of Oren. Claire also noted that Oren's dad was sitting at the back of the church. He was very gaunt and pale, and just stared out of the window.

Claire took a deep breath and began her eulogy, which was read from a paper as she prepared it the night before.

"I met Oren when we were resident doctors. It was more years ago than I care to remember. I was always the party animal and he was the serious one who forced me to study and go to bed at a decent time." Claire looked around and most people just stared at her blankly. She looked down at her paper and continued.

"He was a very dedicated doctor who cared for his patients dearly. He was heavily involved with Doctors without Borders and travelled to many countries, mostly in sub-Sahara Africa. Not only did he train many doctors in those poor countries, but he also saved many people's lives including children."

Claire caught a few people rolling their eyes and she swore others were just looking at her in disgust.

"Oh fuck it," Claire said out loud and she crumpled up the paper and threw it on the ground.

She sheepishly looked at the vicar. "Sorry."

"I would like to believe that most of you think my eulogy is lame, but I don't think that's it. Why are you even here if you don't want to hear about the good things that Oren has done?"

Claire looked around the room. "I know that in the last few months Oren has done some bad things, but we don't know why; and I don't know about you, but I think it was clearly out of character. Something happened and the police are currently investigating it. So don't be so damn judgemental."

Megs got out of her chair and stood next to Claire grabbing her hand.

"Claire's right. I'm here because for nearly four years my relationship with Oren was beautiful. We were supposed to get married in a few months. And since Oren is dead now that is how I want to remember him as my wonderful fiancé."

Claire noticed that a few people started wiping tears from their eyes.

"I can't forgive him for what he did to me, but I can reassure you that that wasn't him. It was his body, but it wasn't his spirit. I don't know what happened and we may never find out. I'm at his funeral because I want to remember the good things. And if I can do that then all of you can, too, as I'm the only true victim here."

Megs abruptly walked back to her chair and Claire followed suit.

The silence within the church was uncomfortable, but without enduring it for too long the vicar was at the podium and he led everyone in a prayer.

*****

Claire didn't think many people would have stayed for the wake, but most did. The sandwiches were barely touched, but a few people did buy drinks. Even Megs was nursing a glass of wine.

Claire sat down next to Megs. "You okay?"

"Not really. Just want this day to end."

214

"You and me both."

"Thanks for doing Oren's eulogy. That was a tough crowd out there."

"It was awful. You totally put them in their place Megs."

"I was just as pissed off as you were. I didn't even know half of them, so I don't think they were there to support me."

"Perhaps they were just curious?" Claire suggested.

"More like nosey bastards."

Claire smiled. "Most likely. It's going to be hard to move forward, eh?"

"I'm moving away Claire."

Claire was surprised. "For good?"

"I'm moving to Toronto."

"Why?"

"Initially I'm moving in with my aunt. Once my business is sold here I'm going to start a little flower shop and cafe in the Toronto area."

"But why are you leaving Vancouver? You love it here."

"It's too painful to stay here."

"I'm going to miss you Megs."

"I know Claire Bear. Keep this information to yourself and please remember to visit me."

Claire gave Megs a hug.

The two women didn't realise that they were being watched.

Outside in the hall Molly, who was wearing a long black leather jacket, a black hat and large sunglasses, was on her cell phone.

"Hey Doug. It's Molly."

"So what's the word?"

"He's dead. I even snuck a peek in the casket."

"Nice work Molly. But you better get out of there before someone recognises you."

Chapter 26

"Sambuca anyone?" There were two left on the tray and Claire downed both and collapsed on her couch laughing.

"Way to go party girl!" Claire's friend Melody shouted as everyone else cheered. House parties at Claire's became a regular occurrence since Megs moved to Toronto a few months ago. And when she wasn't at home partying, she was out at the bars or at someone else's house drinking. Without even realising it, Claire was drinking almost every night.

There was a knock at the door and Melody ran over to open it. A blond-haired stud with dark eyes was at the door. "Come in. We're just getting started."

Melody looked over to Claire and winked. "I want you to meet someone."

"Claire, this is my friend Travis." Claire shook his hand.

"Let's get you a drink," Claire said and she led Travis to her kitchen.

"Beer, wine, rye and coke, Sambuca?" Claire asked.

"Just a beer please," Travis said and smiled at Claire.

"Cheers," Claire said as she hit her glass of rye and coke against Travis' beer.

"So what do you do?" Claire asked.

"I'm a professional skateboarder."

Claire rolled her eyes. "Yeah right!"

"Hey Melody! Come over here for a minute," Travis said.

Melody walked over and it was apparent that she was quite drunk. Her red, curly hair was dishevelled and she could barely walk a straight line. She grabbed onto Travis' arm for support.

"What do I do?" Travis asked Melody.

"He's a skateboarder. And a damned good one at that," Melody said.

"How did you guys meet?" Claire asked.

"I was doing some photo shoots for a friend who was writing an article about Vancouver's skateboarding scene. And Travis was one of the many hot men I got to shoot."

Claire laughed. "Well, next time, invite me along."

Another one of Claire's friends interrupted them. He was holding a plate full of cocaine. "Holey shit. How much is there?"

"About $500 worth. That's what happens when everyone pitches in. And the host gets the first go." Without hesitation Claire snorted a line of coke. Melody and Travis quickly followed suit.

"Nice!" Melody said. "Now we need some more shots of Sambuca."

"There's none left, but I know there's a bottle of tequila floating around," Claire said.

Gnarls Barkley's Crazy started pounding in the background. "Turn it up!" Melody said and she started dancing and grinding with Claire in the kitchen. More people joined them and they all took turns doing shots of tequila.

There was a loud knock at the door.

"Shit. That's a cop knock," Claire said as she turned down the music and answered the door.

Claire was right. Two cops were standing at the door. "Are you Claire Lalonde?"

"Yes," Claire replied.

"This is your fourth warning this month. It's a Tuesday night. It's 1 a.m. We've received four complaints tonight against your address."

"I'm sorry officers. We got carried away. It's my friend's birthday."

The other officer interrupted Claire. "Turn the music down."

"I promise," Claire said.

217

The two cops turned around without saying good-bye and walked down the hall. Claire closed the door.

A couple of her guests grabbed their jackets and put on their shoes. "We gotta go anyways. We're working tomorrow."

More guests followed suit. Soon there was only Melody and Travis left. The three of them were sitting in the living room quietly chatting.

"Melody, you look like you're going to pass out," Claire said.

"I am," Melody replied.

"Here, take the couch. I should go to bed anyways. I'm working tomorrow," Claire said.

Claire helped Melody onto the couch and placed covers over top of her. She made sure that Melody was lying on her side in the recovery position. Even though Claire was extremely intoxicated, she still had enough sense to ensure her friend wouldn't accidentally choke on her own vomit in her sleep. *Another death I'd feel responsible for.* Claire thought to herself.

Claire led Travis into her room and started kissing him. It wasn't long before the two of them were fully naked going at it like rabbits on her bed.

*****

Claire was suddenly awoken by the sound of her alarm clock. Recently she had to change it to the annoying classic beeping noise because she was sleeping through the music that would normally wake her up. Claire was even sleeping through heavy Rage Against the Machine songs.

Claire leaned over and kissed Travis on the cheek. "Thanks for last night," she said.

Travis smiled. "It's early isn't it?"

"I have to go to work, but you can stay here as long as you want. Melody has an extra key."

"Cool," Travis said and he rolled over and passed out again.

Claire's head was banging. She managed to sit on the side of her bed, dressing herself in the same clothes that she wore the day before. Claire then stood up and dizziness overcame her. "Holy shit," she whispered using the walls for support as she walked towards the bathroom.

Claire took a couple of aspirins and washed them down with water. Within seconds she was on her knees throwing up in the toilet bowl.

After vomiting Claire felt a lot better, but her head was still pounding and her body felt like it went through a meat grinder. Claire also felt the aftermath of the copious amount of cocaine she snorted the night before, which made her feel quite depressed.

"Time for the big guns," Claire said to herself.

Claire opened up the bottom drawer and grabbed a bottle of Percocet that she successfully and illegally prescribed to herself. *A perfect mixture of oxycodone and acetaminophen.* Claire thought. She swallowed a couple of pills and sipped some water. She knew what acetaminophen would do to her liver but she didn't care.

Claire was about to brush her teeth, but then remembered her final step of her hangover cure ritual. She put down her toothbrush and walked into the kitchen.

Claire looked around for remnants of any hard liquor. There was about a shot left in the tequila bottle. Without hesitation Claire knocked it back. "Hair of the dog!" Claire said to herself.

She stumbled back into the bathroom and brushed her teeth. She also coated her face with loads of makeup to hide the dark rings underneath her eyes and the red blotches on her face.

Claire walked through the living room and looked over to Melody. Still in the recovery position she was snoring very loudly. Claire put on her boots and left her apartment.

Claire walked over to her car, but couldn't find her car keys in her purse.

"Fuck it," Claire said to herself and walked to the Sky Train station.

The Sky Train was quite packed but she managed to find a seat. Claire kept falling asleep but thankfully they would announce each stop, which would jolt her awake.

When Claire reached her station she found her way out of the Sky Train, pushing her way through people. Claire hated travelling during rush hour, especially when she was fighting a hangover.

"Good morning." One of the resident doctors greeted Claire as she walked through the door.

"Morning," Claire said and walked straight into her office without even looking at the resident doctor.

Claire sat on her chair behind her desk. She became very dizzy and the feeling of tiredness overcame her. She slumped to the side and slid off her chair and onto the floor.

About 30 minutes passed by before one of the nurses was knocking at the door. The waiting room was getting full and the resident doctor couldn't handle all the patients by himself, so he asked the nurse to see when Dr. Lalonde would start taking some patients.

The nurse gently knocked on the office door. "Dr. Lalonde." There was no answer so the nurse knocked even louder. "Dr. Lalonde." The nurse sensed that something was wrong and she tried opening the door, but it was locked.

The nurse ran over to the resident doctor who was about to see a patient that was waiting in one of the treatment rooms. "She's not responding and she locked herself in."

Without hesitation the resident doctor kicked the door in. He ran over to Claire and checked her vitals. He looked up at the nurse. "She's passed out and may have hit her head. Call 911. She needs to go to emergency straight away."

*****

Claire slowly opened her eyes, initially thinking she was at home in bed. As her eyes adjusted she slowly realised that she was in a hospital room. In a confused state she looked down and saw that she was connected to an IV. She looked at the bag that was full of water. "Rehydration therapy?" she said to herself. Puzzled with what happened, she started to press the buzzer at the side of her bed.

A dark-haired man in his mid-40s came into her room within the minute. He smiled at her. Claire assumed that he was a nurse.

"You're awake," he said.

"What am I doing here?" Claire asked.

"You passed out at work. They couldn't wake you up."

All of a sudden memories of the morning started to flood back.

"You need to eat. We'll send some food over to you," the nurse said.

"How long am I going to be here for?" Claire asked.

"One of the doctors will speak to you shortly." And the nurse smiled and walked out of her room.

Claire lied back down and closed her eyes. She couldn't help but think she was in a lot of trouble. They surely took blood samples.

Claire looked out the window and it was light outside. She guessed it was midday.

She heard a very familiar voice outside of her room, but she couldn't pinpoint it. She strained to hear the conversation as she sensed that they were talking about her, but she couldn't make out a thing. After a few minutes a man nearly of retirement age with a grey beard to match his grey hair entered the room holding a tray of food. He was all too familiar to Claire. During her addictions courses he was the lead instructor. He worked with patients from Downtown Eastside for the majority of his career and was mostly known for his treatment of pregnant women who were addicted to drugs and alcohol. He was highly respected in his field.

"Hi Dr. Andrews," Claire said.

Dr. Andrews placed the tray on the side table.

"Good morning Dr. Lalonde."

"Please just call me Claire."

"Okay Claire. How are you feeling?"

"Better than a few hours ago."

"Do you know how long you were out for?"

Claire shrugged her shoulders. "A few hours."

"Try just over 24 hours."

"Jesus!" Claire was shocked.

"We ran some tests and we found some interesting stuff in your blood."

Claire closed her eyes to try and hold back her tears.

"Good thing you didn't drive to work because your blood alcohol level was too high. There were also traces of cocaine in your blood, but what worried me the most was the oxycodone."

Claire couldn't keep her tears back any longer.

Dr. Andrews grabbed the box of tissues and handed it to Claire.

"I'm sure you know the dangers of mixing that drug with alcohol."

"I guess I didn't realise that I still had that much alcohol in my system," Claire said.

"And I can only assume how you got your hands on oxycodone."

Claire was lost for words and just stared out the window.

After a minute of silence Dr. Andrews continued. "I went over your file and spoke to some of your colleagues. I understand that you are dealing with a loss of a very good friend. But it still doesn't excuse the fact that you went to work when you were impaired."

Claire knew what was coming next.

"I'm sorry, but I sent a recommendation to the College of Physicians and Surgeons of BC to suspend your license."

Claire started to cry again.

"Look Claire. I'm not here to lecture you; I'm here to help you. Instead of turning to a shrink to help you deal with such a tragic loss you turned to drugs. And while you are getting treatment you cannot practice medicine. This isn't the first time that I had to treat a doctor. Doctors are actually the worst culprits because they can easily access narcotics."

Claire nodded in agreement.

"We must be honest with each other. While you are recovering in the hospital, I would like you to find some time to write down how long your drug abuse has been going on; and also what drugs you have been taking. I need to get an idea of the magnitude of the situation."

In a way Claire felt relieved. She was getting much needed help and because this was an addiction she wouldn't necessarily lose her license. *A grain of hope*. Claire thought to herself.

"There's just one more thing Claire that I must warn you about. The police are involved. They will be interviewing you today. Can you handle that?"

"Not really," Claire replied.

"Should I tell them to come another day?"

"Tomorrow will be no better than today. I'll never be ready for them."

"So you'll see them today then?"

"Sure."

"Okay. I will see you later Claire."

Claire nodded and put her head back on her pillow.

She looked over at her food, but she didn't have an appetite. She lifted the lid and it was just soup and crackers. Claire remembered that she was out of it for a day and decided that she should eat. It was just chicken noodle soup anyways.

*****

Claire was dozing when a nurse came in. "Dr. Lalonde. A couple of police officers are here to see you."

Claire sat up, and to her surprise Evan walked in. The other officer stayed outside of the room.

Evan grabbed a chair and sat it next to Claire's bed. "How are you feeling?"

"Like shit," Claire said.

"Look, I'm sorry, but this will have to be quick before we do all the formal stuff. We have to arrest you, but not until you are officially released from the hospital."

"What?" Claire said.

"Your colleagues at the clinic suspected that you were stealing narcotics for weeks and they reported it to us this morning."

"Do they have any proof?" Claire asked.

"It gets worse Claire."

"We were also in the middle of investigating a report made by a pharmacist who suspected that you were illegally writing fake prescriptions for yourself. And that's fraud Claire."

Claire lied back down on the bed and closed her eyes.

Evan took her hand. "You have been through so much Claire. And I'm going to try everything in my power get you off lightly."

Claire opened her eyes and looked at Evan. "I wasn't careful when I wrote out those prescriptions because I didn't care. I wanted to get caught. I guess it was a cry for help, but I was too damn stubborn to admit it and see a shrink."

It was quite obvious to Evan that Claire had hit rock bottom.

"Look. I'm going to pretend that you didn't just admit that you wrote out those prescriptions. I only want you to speak to a lawyer and no one else, including me."

Claire nodded.

"Now I'm going to read your arrest caution." Evan looked over to the door. "Hey Ernie. Can you come in here for a minute?"

Evan looked at Claire. "You are under arrest for fraud, do you understand?"

"Yes," Claire replied.

As Evan continued reciting the arrest caution Claire's mind started to wander. *In comparison to Oren I'm getting off lightly.* She thought to herself.

Claire snapped back into the present as Evan touched her leg.

"A police officer will be assigned to stay outside of your hospital room while you recover."

"Why?" Claire asked.

"It's protocol."

Claire nodded and closed her eyes.

"Of course, just in case I try to run away," Claire said.

"I'll see you later. Try to take it easy," Evan said.

Claire didn't say a word and kept her eyes shut until her room was empty.

Chapter 27

Claire was in the hospital for a few more days before being discharged. She believed that they were giving her more than enough time to recover since this was her last bit of freedom before going to jail.

After getting dressed she was handcuffed and escorted out of the hospital. The police officers put her in the back of the cruiser and drove off. The last time she was in a police car was when she was going to the hospital to identify Oren's body. *This time it's not as bad.* Claire thought to herself.

When they arrived at the police station Claire was escorted into the building and was processed right away. She was fingerprinted and her mug shot was taken. Claire was expecting to be placed in a jail cell once all the formalities were conducted, but instead they brought her to a room.

Claire cautiously entered the room and stopped short. Claire's parents were sitting next to a man that she assumed to be a lawyer.

Claire's mother stood up right away and gave her daughter a huge hug. "We just got here this morning. We didn't realise that you were in the hospital."

"How did you know?"

"A very nice police officer called Evan Mazis phoned us up a few days ago and told us everything. Your father and I are here for you my darling."

"You didn't have to fly all the way from Montreal."

"Of course we did. You have no one here and you need our help."

Claire could tell that her father was disappointed in her.

"Sorry Dad," Claire said. But he stayed silent.

"Please take a seat," the lawyer said to the two ladies.

"I'm Daniel McCain. I am actually an old friend of your father's."

Of course. Claire thought to herself.

"I would like to represent you," Daniel said.

Claire nodded.

"So I presume that's a yes."

"Yes," Claire said.

"Well, first things first. Your charges aren't as bad as I was expecting."

"What do you mean?" Claire asked.

"You're being charged for fraud under $5000, which means you are only looking at either six months in jail or a $5000 fine if you are found guilty."

"How's that a good thing?"

"When I first heard your story I was assuming that this would be classified as an indictable offense."

"Which means?"

"Well, if found guilty your minimum sentence would be two years in prison. Thank the Harper Government for the mandatory minimum sentences. It doesn't give judges much flexibility especially since this is your first offense."

Claire was surprised. "Oh my god. Two years?"

Then it dawned on her, Evan must have influenced this decision.

"Next question. Are you going to plead guilty or not-guilty?" Daniel asked.

Claire thought about it for a minute and looked directly at her father. "Guilty."

Claire's father didn't flinch.

"That will make the judge happier and hopefully he or she will give you the more lenient sentence," Daniel said.

"So what's next? Do I go to jail until bail is paid or something?" Claire asked.

"Nope. Because we are dealing with a summary offense you are being released on an appearance notice."

Claire looked confused.

"In other words, you can go home until you are summoned to go to court. They'll send me a letter and I'll let you know right away. Until then you cannot leave the country. I also highly recommend that you stay away from drinking and drugs."

"How long do I have to wait?"

"Probably within the month. And because you are pleading guilty the judge will probably sentence you straight away. It will save them both time and money."

"Claire darling, I'm going to be staying with you throughout this whole awful process. Unfortunately, your father must go home."

"So you're going to babysit me?"

"Claire. You need as much support as possible."

Daniel interrupted. "I highly recommend that your mother stays with you. It shows that you are trying to get as much help as possible for your addiction. I'm going to have to play the sympathy card with the judge."

Claire knew exactly what Daniel was talking about. When Claire was feeling sorry for herself in the hospital she wanted to go to jail, but after it became a potential reality she changed her mind. Claire shook her head. "Jail will not help me."

Daniel looked directly at Claire. "And I'm going to do everything I can to stop that from happening."

"Thank you," Claire said.

Daniel leaned over the table and shook Claire's hand. "I'll be in touch soon."

Claire left the police station with her parents. Her father drove a rented car and Claire sat in the back without saying a word.

"How many bedrooms does your apartment have?" Claire's mother asked.

"Two. I have a futon in the spare room. It's comfy."

"Your father will be staying here for another few days. We would rather stay with you than in a hotel room."

"That's fine, but my house is a mess."

"I'll help you clean it."

"Please don't mom. There's a really good Thai restaurant a couple of blocks away from my apartment. I'll clean up while you two eat."

"You need to eat, too," Claire's mother said.

"Can you bring me back a Thai green curry?"

"Absolutely."

Claire's parents parked their car and escorted her into the apartment.

"Brace yourselves," Claire said as she opened the door.

The smell of stale food and booze wafted out of the apartment.

"Jesus, Claire." Those were the first words her father uttered to her all day.

"I told you so," Claire said.

Claire's parents entered her apartment and looked around. "Nice apartment if it wasn't for the mess."

"Thanks mom."

"Well, it looks like you'll need a couple of hours at least."

"Yes mom."

Claire's mother gave her daughter a hug. "Thai green curry with chicken?"

"Yeah. Thanks," Claire said. And her parents left the apartment.

Claire closed the door and looked around. There were bottles of booze everywhere and her kitchen counter was full of take-out containers. For the past week while she was in the hospital they were just festering. Claire took a large garbage bag and threw everything in there. At that point she didn't even care about recycling.

She was about to open up her refrigerator when a photo being held up by a magnet caught her eye. It was a photo of her, Megs and Oren sticking out their tongues on top of Blackcomb Mountain in Whistler. It was a couple of winters ago when Megs and Oren went skiing with Claire and one of her ex-boyfriends. And the ex-boyfriend was actually the one who took the photo. "Before everything went to shit," Claire said out loud and took the photo down. She was about to throw it into the garbage, but couldn't go through with it. Instead she put it into one of her kitchen drawers. The memory was too painful.

Claire managed to fill up two large garbage bags full of booze bottles, beer cans and take-away containers.

She hauled them out of her apartment and threw them into the dumpster. She then noticed, out of the corner of her eye, a black SUV parked on the same block. She slowly looked over and noticed someone sitting in the driver's seat.

Her heart started pounding as she was sure it was the drug cartel. She was certain that they were going to kill her, especially since she's been arrested and was dealing with the police.

"Fuck it," Claire said out loud. She was fed up of being afraid and decided to confront the individual who was watching her.

She started walking towards the SUV, slowly at first, but then gaining speed as she got closer and closer.

Claire heard a door from the adjacent house open and slam shut. A young girl with her younger brother in tow ran up to the SUV. Claire stopped in her tracks and watched a father help his two kids into the vehicle.

Claire felt stupid as she let paranoia get the better of her. She walked back to her apartment and slammed the door shut.

As she walked back into the kitchen her heart stopped. There was a note on the fridge, where the picture used to be not even five minutes ago, which said. "Say anything to the police and you will die."

The thought that someone was in her house only moments before made her feel sick. She took the note off of the fridge, crumpled it up and threw it in the garbage.

Claire then collapsed on the couch and started crying.

Chapter 28

Two weeks after Claire received the note courtesy of Doug, she was sitting in a court- room waiting for the judge to sentence her. She also had to admit, Daniel did a good job representing her. Claire didn't even have to say a thing. And the judge even praised her for admitting herself to a drug rehabilitation program.

Claire was relieved that she was only fined. However, the judge also ordered her to carry out 100 hours of community service at the Downtown Eastside Women's Centre.

After Claire left the courtroom her mother gave her a huge hug. "I'm so relieved. I couldn't handle you being in jail."

"Me neither," Claire said.

Claire turned to Daniel and shook his hand. "Thank you!"

"That's my job," Daniel said.

"Shouldn't we celebrate?" Claire's mother asked.

"Maybe a quick bite for lunch. I want to go to the Women's Centre this afternoon and sort out this community service business."

"Sounds good," Claire's mother said.

The bailiff closed the courtroom door and watched Claire walk outside with her lawyer and mother. Once they were out of sight he looked around. The courthouse was empty.

He took his cell phone out of his pocket and dialled a number.

"Doug. It's Max."

"What's the news?" Doug asked.

"She was done for fraud. She got caught writing out prescriptions for herself."

Doug was surprised as he thought Claire was more strong-willed than that. "Really?"

"You were never mentioned," Max said.

"So I guess I'll let her live. Cheers," Doug said and he hung up the phone.

*****

Claire was waiting in the Women's Centre for about 45 minutes to meet with one of the social workers. Normally she would have been annoyed, but Claire was fascinated with the comings and goings in the Women's Centre. It was as busy as the hospital's emergency room during its peak hours, and it was full of Vancouver's most vulnerable people. She was amazed at how organised the chaos was and how passionate the workers were.

A short, but tough-looking lady with a blond bob busted into the front door. She walked straight through and entered a room in the back.

A few minutes later the lady returned and she stood in front of Claire.

"Are you the one who was ordered to do community service here?"

Claire stood up and stuck out her hand. "Yes. I'm Claire Lalonde."

The lady grabbed her hand and quickly shook it. "I'm Elizabeth Manning, but please call me Liz. Can you follow me into my office?"

"Sure," Claire said.

Liz closed the door behind Claire and sat at her desk. "Take a seat."

Claire sat down facing Liz. She felt a bit funny being on the other side of a desk.

Liz shuffled some papers and her face became very serious as she looked up to Claire.

"Although the judge wouldn't have ordered you here if she felt you were a risk, but I need to understand your background just to make sure."

Claire nodded.

"What's your story?"

"As in what I've done wrong?"

"Yes."

"Where to begin?" Claire took a deep breath. "I'm a medical doctor. In the last few months a lot of bad things have happened to me and I turned to drugs."

Claire looked at Liz who didn't even flinch.

"You look familiar. Did you go to UBC?" Liz asked.

"Yeah, for med school. I graduated in 2008."

"We would have been there at the same time then," Liz said.

Claire was surprised as Liz looked about 40 or so.

"Well, let's get back to business," Liz said.

"What kind of drugs were you addicted to?"

"Prescription drugs. I self-prescribed mostly opiate-based drugs using pseudonyms and a pharmacist finally caught me."

"Would you consider yourself addicted?"

"I was, but I'm currently in rehab."

"Did you admit yourself?"

"Yes, but it wasn't until I was hospitalised. I mixed alcohol with oxycodone."

"You know, a lot of my girls are addicted to oxycodone."

Claire didn't know what to say.

Liz sat up straight and continued.

"It would be great to have a doctor volunteering here, but I'm assuming that your license was pulled."

"The College of Physicians and Surgeons of BC suspended my license."

"For how long?" Liz asked.

"Until I finish the rehabilitation program."

"Are you on the 12-month program?"

"That is correct," Claire replied.

Liz scribbled a few things down and looked up at Claire. "Excuse my French, but you look like you're getting your shit together."

"I can assure you that I am," Claire said.

"Here's a form that I want you to fill in. It includes a list of volunteer tasks, and I just want you to check the ones you are interested in doing."

Liz handed Claire the form on a clipboard and a pen.

Claire smiled at Liz. "Thanks for not judging me."

Liz looked a bit confused. "I'm a social worker, of course I don't judge."

"I know but..." Claire couldn't finish her sentence.

"You aren't the first doctor that I met who was a drug addict, and you won't be the last. At least you regained control. You know, there are even some doctors who lost their jobs and ended up on the streets because of it," Liz said.

Liz stood up and walked towards the door. "Just fill the form out in here and leave it on my desk. Please close the door when you leave."

"Okay. Thank you," Claire said.

"I'll be touch in a couple of days and we'll sort out your hours," Liz said and she left the room.

Claire quickly filled out the form and left the Women's Centre. She walked down Colombia Street and turned on to East Hastings Street. Claire stopped at Hastings and Main, which also had the unfortunate moniker of Wastings and Pain. Trying not to stare she saw so many people who desperately needed medical assistance. One man even had an open knife wound across his cheek, but he didn't seem to notice.

Not even a month ago she drove down this same street in her fancy BMW, and considered these people a nuisance as they would randomly cross the road like zombies nearly causing accidents. Claire hated herself for thinking this way, especially since she was a physician who was supposed to be compassionate and ethical.

She wondered if any of her illegally prescribed drugs ended up in the hands of any of these individuals. She knew the answer and felt that she owed the community so much. She was no different than Doug. She, too, lived off of other people's pain and suffering. This revelation flooded Claire with emotion. And she realised she had a lot of work to do in order to give back to the community. And the mandatory community service was only just the beginning.

www.ingramcontent.com/pod-product-compliance
Lightning Source LLC
Chambersburg PA
CBHW060135130626
46556CB00006B/2361